I0638927

Harlan County Haunts
And Tales Of The Unusual And Amazing

Featuring

Caroline
From The Journal Of James Saylor

Darla Saylor Jackson

© 2008 by Jackson Publishing

All rights reserved.

ISBN 978-0-6151-9914-6

Printed in the United States of America

Preface

Ghost stories are a part of the mountains and we mountain folk take our ghost stories seriously. The telling of these spooky tales is a part of our culture and an important part of mountain life both past and present. You don't ask someone in the mountains if they believe in ghosts; you ask them how many they've seen. Most stories I heard were finalized by the phrase, "…and that's the honest-to-God's truth." We don't need to make up stories in the mountains; we have far too many true ones to keep us entertained.

This book is a compilation of stories. I call them "stories," but they are really personal accounts. Most of them happened in southeastern Kentucky, mainly Harlan County. Not all the stories happened in Harlan or even in Kentucky, but they all have a Kentucky connection. The main criteria for the stories I have written is that they must be true. I believe all my contributors to be extremely credible.

Some of the tales are from my childhood or from others' childhoods, but once again, they had to be true and from a credible source. I am often asked if I have frequent supernatural experiences and the answer is no. My encounters with the unexplained are few and far between and that is the way I like it. There are only a couple of times in this book where I speak of my own experiences.

My inspiration for writing this book was the feature story, "Caroline." It was the first story written. I soon realized that it could not be a book by itself due to its length, so I created this book to feature it.

Soon after I began interviewing contributors, I began receiving stories that were not ghostly in nature, but rather inspirational or religious. I found these just as intriguing as the scary stuff, so I decided this should be a book for all unusual experiences, not just ghostly. In this book, you will find monsters, creatures, the creepy, the weird, out of body experiences, psychic experiences, encounters with the afterlife, angels, demons, and of course, lots of ghosts.

While reading this book, in addition to experiencing the unexplained, I hope you experience mountain life and mountain people; the way they were and the way they are today.

Acknowledgements

I would like to thank my son, Holden, and my husband, Dewayne, for their constant support of me and this project.

I would like to thank my parents, Darlene and Kale Saylor, Jr., and my uncle, Stratton Saylor, for their help in "rounding up" stories.

A huge thanks to Darlene Steele, who started out as a contributor, but ended up much more than that. She found many sources, helped with the photographs, and helped with the entire book.

To my uncle, James Saylor, more gratitude than can be expressed. He experienced "Caroline" and allowed me to share.

To my aunt, Loretta Martin, much love and thanks for diving in wholeheartedly to this project and giving undying dedication to it.

This book is dedicated to:
Dewayne, Holden, and my family, especially James and Loretta.

My nation, my people, the Piqua Shawnee.

All the people who shared and contributed.

My cousin, Ken Tankersley, who, after two hours of listening to me one winter night said, "That's a book!" I will forever be indebted to him for all he has done and continues to do.

My dear friend, Judy Sizemore, who makes me a better person just by being in her presence.

My friends who forever inspire me: Migali, Nicki, Jennifer, Alfredo, Betty, Mike, Gayla, Susan, and all the artists of the Kentucky Arts Council, especially Dianne, Russ, and Angelyn.

The unidentified girl whose body was found on Pine Mountain in 1969. Someone is still trying.

Contents

I wanted this to be the first story in the book because it contains the first ghost story I ever heard and also, the single most terrifying thing that ever happened to me. This story is dedicated to the memory of my beloved grandparents, Isaiah and Mossie Saylor.

The Two Stories

My grandmother was a simple honest woman who rarely spoke. When she did speak, it was important and what she spoke was the truth. She was not a great storyteller like my grandfather. He, on the other hand, could tell incredible stories as long as he had willing listeners. I remember my grandmother telling only one story. It didn't start out as a story; she was simply telling of something that she could not explain. It turned into a story because it was so interesting. I would ask her to tell it over and over again. It wasn't scary - just fascinating. Most importantly, because she was telling it, I knew it was the truth.

I have only one story that is from my own personal experience. Some people go through life having bizarre unexplained incidences, but I don't. I have just one story. It's not only my story... it is my grandparents' story, too. I am the only one who is still alive to tell it. My grandparents experienced both of these events, and even though they happened over forty years apart, I feel they may somehow be related.

My maternal grandmother was Mossie Mosley Saylor. I called her Susie, as did a lot of other people. My grandfather, Isaiah, gave her that nickname. My grandparents were married in the 1930s. My grandfather was a bit older than my grandmother. Susie was only a teenager when she married my grandfather. They had both been raised in Leslie County, Kentucky, in small mountain communities. My grandfather was from Middle Fork and Susie was from Philip's Fork (pronounced Fip-sis Fork).

When Papaw and Susie were wed, they moved to an area of Harlan County called Straight Creek. Straight Creek was known as an area where it was okay to be Indian, it was okay to be white, and it was okay for whites to marry Indians. This was not an issue for Papaw and Susie. They were both a Cherokee-white mix, so they fit in well.

Papaw built a small cabin on Straight Creek (you are never "at" or "in" Straight Creek, you are always "on" Straight Creek). The cabin seemed to be on the verge of being a shack, but that was the best they could do at the time. The cabin had a dirt floor and no doors or windows. There were quilts hanging where doors and windows should have been. The quilts kept out rain, drafts, and animals. Running water and electricity were both unheard of in that area at that time. Lanterns were used for light and the Straight Creek of the Cumberland River was used for water.

To make a living, Papaw went into the logging business and soon he had other men working with him. Susie would cook dinner for all of them. Her "kitchen" was outside. She had to pack water to cook, wash dishes, wash clothes, drink, bathe, etc. Susie made her kitchen as close to the creek as possible without getting too far away from the cabin.

Every evening, Susie prepared dinner, and when it began to get dark, the loggers would come and eat. After dinner, they would stay awhile and discuss the events of the day or make plans for the next. While they were inside talking, Susie would go outside and wash dishes in a big metal tub. On cloudy nights she needed a lantern, but on clear nights she could see by the light of the moon. Most nights, her cooking fire would still be burning. It wasn't long into this routine when something unusual began to happen. From far off in the distance, Susie could hear people traveling on the dirt road that passed by the cabin. She could hear laughter and talking from both men and women. She described them as "a whole passel of people," which was mountain brogue for "a large group of people." The people would get closer and closer until finally they were right in front of the cabin, but she could see no one. They were so close that she could hear their feet hitting the ground as they walked, but no one was there. The group would pass right by her, and she could hear them continue on down the road until they were too far away to be heard. It was not unusual for groups of people to pass by on the road at night, so the first time she heard it she paid no attention to it. She assumed that they were coming home from church and waited for them to pass to see if she knew them. The invisible people passed by every night. One night after a long, hard day, the loggers didn't stay around after dinner to chat. Papaw was alone in the cabin when Susie heard the people coming. She ran in the cabin and got Papaw. She wanted to see if she was the only one who could hear them. She was not. He could hear them, too.

Some nights, the crowd of people was lively and cheerful. Other nights, there was a solemn mood about them. Susie said that she would get very quiet and listen to them and she could actually hear some of their conversations. She said, on one occasion, they were talking about a preacher. Susie said that sometimes the bright moon lit everything up like daylight and sometimes the fire would light up the yard and the dirt road. Still, she never saw a single person.

One night as Susie washed dishes, a ball of fire shot up out of the ground. It began moving in large circles all over the yard. Finally, it quit circling and made a straight line toward her. She said she was too shocked to move. It came right up to the tip of her shoes and then disappeared back into the ground at her feet. The group of people did not pass by that night. The next morning, she went out to see if there were burned places on the ground, but there was nothing there.

Time went on, and the logging business was doing well. Soon, Papaw and Susie were able to improve their cabin and add on a kitchen. Susie never knew if the invisible people stopped coming or if she could no longer hear them because she wasn't outside at night anymore. Eventually, they built a better house near the spot where the old cabin once stood. Susie spoke of this well into the 1970s. I loved to hear her tell about the unseen people.

I used to have to walk by the place where the old cabin once stood on the way from my parents' house to my grandparents' new house. I often wondered what would happen if I stopped and waited until nightfall. Would I be able to hear the people, too? I was never brave enough to find out. If the sun was going down, I would hurry by quickly. Sometimes, I would sing loudly so there would be no way I could hear them. The old barn stood until the mid-1970s. One day, it burned down for no reason. I wondered if the ball of fire had caused it. That place was halfway between my parents' house and Papaw and Susie's. Sometimes, even in the bright sunlight, I would get an uneasy feeling there and break into a swift run. I always blamed it on the fact that I wasn't close to either house and somewhat alone, but that wasn't it. There was a heaviness about that place that I can't describe. This exact spot plays a major part in my story.

In the summer of 1982, I was 13 years old. I spent most of my time at Papaw and Susie's. They had just bought a satellite dish, and for people who had only gotten one channel, NBC, for years and then finally, ABC and CBS, well, this was a big deal. I would sit up nearly all night and watch movies, which were another thing we weren't accustomed to. Harlan's theater had recently closed and the nearest movie theater at that time was either in Dryden, Virginia, or Corbin, Kentucky. Both were close to two hours away. Satellites were the biggest thing to hit Straight Creek since they came and paved the road.

It was a Saturday night, and as usual, I was going to stay up late and watch movies. I told Susie that I would be sleeping on the couch. She wanted to make me a "pallet" (makeshift bed) on the floor, but I told her to give me a blanket and pillow and I'd be fine. Papaw and Susie went to bed and I was in the living room. The only light in the house was from the television I was watching.

Susie didn't allow lights on after dark, which defeats the purpose of having lights, really. She was always convinced that someone was trying to shoot into the house. She thought that if a light was on, the shooter could see you and you could become a target. We had to see by the light of the television, and if you were in a bedroom that didn't face the road, you could turn on a lamp. If the television was off, you could turn on a small lamp in the living room if it was really necessary. I can rarely remember the ceiling lights ever being on. We pretty much walked around in the dark.

That particular night, my grandparents went to bed at 11:00 pm. I'm not sure what time I decided to sleep, but it must have been sometime around 2:00 am Since this was in the days before remote controls, I got up, walked across the room, and turned off the television. I stood there for a minute and let my eyes adjust to the dark before I attempted to make my way back to the couch.

Within a few seconds, I could see pretty well due to a full moon and a large window that Susie referred to as "the picture window." I, of course, did not turn on any lights to make my way back to the couch, especially since I was in the living room. This room faced the road, and the picture window was Susie's greatest concern regarding "the shooter." We passed by that window with great caution. It was a big window and its only covering was some sheer curtains. I walked back to the couch and lay down.

Moonlight now flooded the room and I could see really well. I didn't close my eyes; I was enjoying the soft glow in the room. There were open windows throughout the house to let the night breeze in. I could hear crickets, frogs, and an occasional whippoorwill. These were my favorite sounds in the world. The room was a bit too warm, and I wished I could turn on the air conditioner in the kitchen. Susie wasn't afraid of air conditioning, just a bit suspicious of it. It could never be on "unattended" and could never be turned on at night. A yellow electric fan could be used at night, and I heard its soft humming in the kitchen.

Another light entered the room. It appeared to be headlights from a car passing by the house, but the light was moving unusually slow for a car. I listened, but couldn't hear a car motor. I lay still and watched. The light came to a stop right in front of the house. I immediately rolled off of the couch and landed on my hands and knees. I thought to myself, "Susie's been right all these years! Someone is trying to shoot into the house!"

I began to crawl across the room toward the hall so I could alert my grandparents. I kept really low as I passed the picture window and didn't dare rise up to look out. The light began to move again. It was continuing down the road at the same slow pace. I was glad it was leaving, but I still felt I should tell Papaw and Susie about it. Now the light was no longer in the room. I decided it was safe to peek out the window. I crawled over to it and slowly rose up. The light was stopped at the place where my grandparents' old cabin had been, very near my Aunt Loretta's house. I could barely see it. I don't know if it disappeared or moved out of sight, but soon it was no longer visible. I now debated waking my grandparents.

I noticed something different as I stared out the window. All the sounds of the night were gone. It was totally silent except for the humming of the fan. The animals outside were now quiet.

Suddenly, out of dead silence came sheer chaos. A deafening booming noise sent me standing straight up. The room was now filled with percussion and human voices. It seemed to come from everywhere and was so loud I could feel it in my head and chest. I quickly began running toward my grandparents' room. My legs were trembling so much that I didn't have good control of them. I met the silhouette of my grandfather in the dark hallway. Susie was behind him. They said nothing and I was unable to speak. I moved aside and let Papaw go past me. He entered the living room and Susie and I closely followed.

Papaw was barefoot and wearing jeans. In his left hand, he was carrying a pistol. He wasn't wearing a shirt and his copper skin glistened in the moonlight. I could see the scar on his chest where he was wounded in the war. It was now obvious that the sounds were coming from outside. Papaw walked to the front door and began unlocking it. I grabbed his arm and begged him not to go outside. My voice came out in high pitched shrieks. Papaw said something back to me, but I couldn't hear him over all the noise. He didn't seem scared at all and was totally emotionless.

He stepped out onto the porch and began walking toward the driveway. Despite being terrified, I could not stand the thought of Papaw going out into the night alone. I went out right behind him. Susie tried to pull me back and we both ended up on the porch. She was scared to death.

Susie stayed on the porch, but I went to the driveway where Papaw was. There was nothing out there, just a lot of noise. As we stood there, I was no longer hysterical like I had been and was able to listen and concentrate. The sound was actually coming from the old house site, just down the road a bit. The booming was the sound of a drum. I could hear wailing and crying from both men and women. I could hear a man's voice above all others. His voice was powerful and clear as he let out melodic cries. His voice was beautiful, but he seemed to be in pain. I could also hear singing, but I couldn't understand any of the words. The singing and crying was coming from at least 50 people.

Then, as suddenly as it began, it ended. We stood there, in the night, in total silence. All I could hear was a dull ringing in my ears. We stood there a few minutes more and then Papaw began walking toward the house. My legs felt weak as I followed him and neither of us spoke. I slept with Susie that night, but neither of us really slept. Sometime that morning, I finally dozed off.

When I awoke, I went into the kitchen where Papaw and Susie were drinking coffee. We did not speak about what happened. I wanted to, but I could tell that they did not. I went into another room and called my aunt. Her house was the closest to the sounds. I asked her what she thought it was and she said that she didn't know what I was talking about. She said that she hadn't heard anything. I then called my parents. Their house was about the same distance away as ours. They heard nothing. All of Straight Creek should have heard that. It was so loud that I heard ringing in my ears for hours after.

That evening, Susie and I did what we did almost every summer evening. We got a quilt, laid it on the grass in the yard, and sat on it. "What do you think that was, Susie?" I asked. She thought for a moment and replied, "I don't know for sure, but I would say it was those people coming back from church." We never spoke of it again.

Isaiah and Mossie Saylor

The Mining Camp

Coal mining camps were communities made by coal companies for their employees to live. These communities usually had small identical houses, built side by side, in long straight rows. In the larger camps, there were churches, possibly a school, and maybe a post office. All mining camps had a commissary, which was basically a general store.

The difference between a general store and a commissary is that the commissaries didn't take regular currency. They took "scrip," which was how the coal miners were paid. All week long, families would get food and other necessities on credit at the commissary. On Fridays, the miners were paid entirely in scrip.

The only place they could spend this was at the commissary, as it was worthless anywhere else. Each coal company had their own scrip, so you couldn't even spend it at another commissary. It didn't matter anyway, by payday it was owed all to the commissary. Families would pay off their debt and it would start all over the following week. At that time, miners were working for food and a place to stay with no hope of bettering themselves or their families. This next story took place at one of these camps.

As a child, my aunt's husband, Rusty, lived in the Green Hill Coal Mining Camp on the Right Fork of Straight Creek in Bell County, Kentucky. One night, tragedy hit the small camp. A house caught on fire and was so quickly consumed by flames that two small children were unable to make it out and both perished. The house suffered extensive damage and stood empty, in need of major repair.

On most summer evenings, families gathered on their small front porches to enjoy the breeze and shade, and to escape their hot houses. This particular summer evening was no exception, and the camp was filled with lighthearted conversation and laughter. Near dusk, the residents of the camp noticed two small children walking down the road. Normally, this would not be unusual. Children were often sent to the commissary to pick up something.

What was so unusual about these two children is that they were the ones who had burned in the house fire. Everyone knew the children and immediately recognized them. People began to stand and walk to the edge of their porches, never taking their eyes off the children. They were all shocked by what they saw. The two siblings, a brother and a sister, walked side by side. They were expressionless and walked along very slowly and steadily. They looked at no one as they passed the houses. Everyone in the camp stared in amazement as the children calmly continued on. The young brother and sister stopped in front of what used to be their house. They turned and walked through the small yard and climbed the steps of the porch. Then, both entered the charred ruins of the house, never to be seen again. The residents of the coal camp stood silently in disbelief.

What happened at this mining camp is very rare. Ghosts are usually witnessed by one person who is left to try to convince others of what they saw. What happened here is called a "group sighting," where many people see the phenomena. The people who lived at the mining camp saw the children do what they did many times while living, as if they wanted to go home one last time.

The Good Spirit And The Bad Spirit

Loyall, Kentucky, is a small community nestled in the mountains of Harlan County. It is not like most mountain communities that have little country roads with farms and houses sparsely scattered here and there. Loyall is one of the little towns that "sprung up" during the coal boom of the earlier part of the twentieth century. During this time, it grew as a large coal shipping center. Loyall has streets and sidewalks with houses placed close together. At one time, Loyall was a thriving community that had shops, a movie theater, restaurants, churches, and its own school. Loyall has now "dried up" somewhat. There are still quite a few people living there and a few places of business and churches, but the school is now closed, as well as the theater, restaurants, and most shops. Loyall is where the next story takes place.

Martha has lived in Loyall for many years. She lives in a house that was built in the 1950s. She hadn't lived there long when she discovered that her house was inhabited by a spirit. Soon after moving there, she began to hear noises. The noises mostly occurred while she was in bed. Often, the noise sounded like a radio on somewhere in the house. After many nights of getting up and checking all the radios and television, Martha realized that the sound must be coming from a different source.

Sometimes she heard talking, while other times she heard footsteps walking around her house. She would usually hear these sounds when she was at the point of falling asleep. It was as if something was trying to aggravate or annoy her. Martha was never scared when these things happened. She wasn't even frightened when she began seeing a dark figure walking by her bed or peering into her window. She could sense that whatever was in her house was "good" and non-threatening. Whatever was there seemed to be mischievous in nature and never really bothered anyone. Even when Martha sensed a presence in the room with her, it never really disturbed her. Martha has lived peacefully with this spirit for a long time and is totally comfortable in her home.

The house next door to Martha's is inhabited by a spirit, too, but that is where the similarity ends. The spirit in this house seems to be malevolent and "dark." Martha was not aware of this spirit until the original owners of the house moved out and her niece moved in. Shortly after moving in, Martha's teenage great-nephew began telling of "something" being in his room. He was very frightened and uncomfortable in his new home. His mother was concerned about his behavior, but had never really experienced anything in the house herself. Martha was visiting one day and asked her nephew to describe what was in his room. He said that he immediately sensed something was with him the first day he moved there. At first, it was just something he sensed, but it didn't take long before he began physically feeling it. He said that one night while he was lying in bed, unseen hands began pushing him down into the mattress. Finally, something actually lay down on top of him, preventing him from moving or getting up. It eventually disappeared.

Martha asked her nephew to take her to his room. As they entered, she could tell that there was a different atmosphere there. She went over to his bed and lay down. She could feel something pressing down on her! Startled, she quickly got up. As she stood there, she felt something "dark" was all around. She sensed evil. She told her niece that something must be done to rid the home of this sinister presence.

Martha's niece called her preacher. She told him about her son and his fear of the new home. She asked him if he could bless their home and cleanse it of any evil presence. The preacher agreed and came to the house the next day. Martha could tell that the preacher was in doubt that an evil presence existed. He acted in a very patronizing manner, and she could tell that he thought he was in the home of a mother and son who were tense about moving to a new place. He did not sincerely believe that evil was there and was using this as an opportunity to try to sway the young man away from rock music, which he felt was much more evil than any ghost.

He told the teenager that the evil was in his room because of the posters of rock groups he had hanging all over the walls. Then the preacher told him that the spirit could not leave due to all the sinful artwork that covered his walls and that he must take them down and burn them all. The young boy did just that. He and his mother immediately began ripping them down. Once the walls were bare, they then went to the backyard and burned them. The preacher delighted in this, but Martha knew that none of this was going to help with the evil that dwell in the home.

Only a few days after the blessing of the home, strange things began happening again. This time, it was more aggressive and angry. The young boy began to be struck by an unseen force. He was slapped, hit, and pushed. Once, he was nearly pushed down the stairs. He was forced down in his mattress so hard, that on different occasions, his body actually left an imprint in it. His mother began being tripped by something and several times fell to the floor. Needless to say, Martha's niece and great-nephew did not live in the house for very long. After a short time of living there, they put the home up for sale and moved out.

An older couple bought the house. Martha became friends with them, but never mentioned what had happened to her niece and nephew or why they moved. She didn't want the couple to be frightened and hoped that the spirit was gone. Martha had speculated that the activity experienced in the house by her niece and nephew was the result of her nephew's friend that frequently visited the home. Martha didn't like her nephew's friend at all. She had heard that the boy was dabbling in the occult and satanic worship. When she looked into his eyes, she could see a certain amount of evil in them. Maybe since he was gone, so was the spirit.

Time passed, and the couple seemed content. One day, out of the blue, they came to Martha's house and announced that they were moving in two weeks. Martha was shocked and asked why they were leaving. They told her that they could not endure living in the home anymore. They said that they never spoke of what was going on inside their house in fear of sounding insane.

They began to tell of things that were happening in the house that was all too familiar to Martha. They told of being pushed and pressed down onto their bed. Their bedroom was the same one that had been Martha's nephew's room. The man described how he was nearly pushed down the stairs. They also told of something that had never happened to Martha or her niece and nephew. They had seen it! Many times they witnessed a black figure lurking in the house. Once, as the man was coming down the stairs, the dark figure passed by him going up the stairs! That had been the final straw. As soon as the entity began manifesting itself, they knew it was time to go.

The couple was not interested in selling the house; they were only interested in leaving. They gave Martha a key to it just in case she ever needed in and asked her to check on it occasionally. Martha wasn't all that anxious to go back into the house, but agreed that she would keep an eye on it for them.

No one lives there now - no one except the dark presence that scares everyone away. It is still there. Martha feels it and sees it from time to time when she has to go in the empty house. Her granddaughter was visiting one day and told Martha that she wanted to go to the "haunted house" and see the ghost. Martha told her that ghosts didn't show up on command, but reluctantly got the key and went next door. They went in and walked around slowly. They were standing in the dining room when both of them looked toward the stairway. Both of them caught a glimpse of a black figure peeking around the corner. Martha and her granddaughter left the house very quickly.

According to Martha, the spirit is there and is getting stronger. What was, at first, a "presence" or a feeling soon turned into something you could physically feel. Then, according to the couple, it turned into something shapeless you could see, and now it is a full body apparition. What's next? Martha says it is becoming quite the show-off and appears any time anyone wants it to. Martha told me that I am more than welcome to come and take a look for myself. I haven't yet decided...

Coman And Carrie

In most places, when someone is described as "scary," it means that they are frightening. In the mountains, if someone is described as "scary," it means they are easily frightened. My paternal grandfather's sister and brother-in-law were very scary people. Their names were Coman and Carrie, and Coman seemed to be the scarier of the two.

Coman was scared to death of the Honey Branch Cemetery at Middle Fork in Leslie County, Kentucky. He claimed to have seen lights in the cemetery, late at night, when no one was there. He so greatly feared passing Honey Branch at night that he always carried an empty sack with him. As he neared the cemetery, he would fill the sack with rocks. He would then pay one of the neighborhood boys to carry his "groceries" home for him. As soon as he and the boy passed the cemetery, Coman would suddenly get a burst of energy. He would tell the boy that he could carry his groceries home, pay the boy a dollar, and then empty the rocks from the sack and place it back in his pocket for his next trip by the cemetery. In defense of Coman, one other person claims to have seen lights in the Honey Branch Cemetery late at night when he was absolutely certain no one was there, and this person is not scary at all.

Much to their terror, Coman and Carrie's house acquired a ghost. They had lived there for years with no trouble, but one day a ghost just popped right in and decided to stay. Coman and Carrie were in great distress regarding their new haunting. Needless to say, they were afraid to spend nights at their house. They needed a safe place to stay, so they decided that the best thing to do was sleep in their car in the parking lot of my grandfather's church.

My paternal grandfather was a Holiness preacher. Every night after nightfall, Coman and Carrie pulled into the church's small parking lot. They parked, went to sleep, and the next morning, they drove home. This became a regular occurrence. Like most other Pentecostal churches, services were held at night. The only time a Sunday morning service was held was when something happened called a "5th Sunday." If a month had five Sundays versus four, on the fifth one, there would be a morning service that lasted most of the day. On church nights, Coman and Carrie attended the service and afterward, get in their car and go to sleep.

My grandfather lived on the hill above the church. He had 12 children, and the temptation to "mess" with Coman and Carrie was far too tempting for at least one of them. After church services one night, my Uncle Kenneth sneaked back inside the church. He dragged and knocked the pews around in a way that made a horrible noise. This frightened Coman and Carrie so much that they quickly drove away and found another parking spot to spend the night.

One night, after Coman and Carrie's arrival, my uncle got the family dog and wrapped it up in a large sheet. He took it to the church parking lot and turned it loose. The dog, which had trouble seeing, began to run wildly and aimlessly through the parking lot. Coman and Carrie were not yet asleep, so they peered through the car windows to see what the commotion was about.

Coman took one look at this big white thing running around and panicked. He turned on the ignition, stepped on the gas, and sped out of the parking lot in a cloud of dust and gravel. They had gone no more than a hundred feet when they wrecked in a ditch. When my dad awoke very early the next morning to go squirrel hunting, on his way he noticed Coman and Carrie's car in the ditch and went to see about it. Upon further inspection, he discovered them sound asleep in it. My dad didn't bother to wake them. On his way back home, he saw that they had gotten their car out of the ditch and had gone home to spend the day with their ghost.

After the "dog incident," Coman and Carrie selected other parking spots and began rotating their nights at each spot, so perhaps the ghosts and spirits wouldn't find them so predictable. Coman and Carrie waited a long time for their ghost to leave. When it didn't, they did. After many nights sleeping in a car and many days living with a ghost, Coman and Carrie finally decided to move. They moved to another house and apparently, never had any more ghost problems because they were never seen sleeping in their car after that.

Honey Branch Cemetery - Saylor, Leslie Co., KY

The Little People Of Stone Mountain

In Cherokee folklore, there are many stories about the Aniyvwi Tsunsdi (ah-nee-yuh-wee choon - stee) or Little People. The Little People are handsome and about knee-high. They help those who are lost and lend a hand when needed. They are very private and do not want the location of their villages disclosed. It is also said that they put curses on those who tell the location of their homes, and if you do not ask their permission before taking something out of the woods, they may get mischievous.

Supposedly, there is a secret village of the Aniyvwi Tsundsdi in Whitley County, Kentucky, near Cumberland Falls. Rich in Cherokee heritage, Harlan County has its own stories of Little People that live in Pine Mountain and in Stone Mountain near Lee County, Virginia. My husband, Dewayne, had a grandfather who was one-half Cherokee. His name was Oney Jackson, and his name is a corruption of the Cherokee word for "bear," which is Yona or Yoni.

Oney would tell about "dwarfs" that lived in Stone Mountain. He would tell Dewayne to always watch out for them and to never follow them. One day, while Dewayne and Papaw Oney were squirrel hunting in Stone Mountain, Papaw Oney said, "Wait! Don't go any farther. We are getting close to where the little dwarfs live. If someone gets too close they'll leave and not come back." Papaw Oney often spoke of little people living all over Stone Mountain.

Dewayne spent much of his teenage years in Stone Mountain. He and his best friend, Steve, camped and hunted almost every weekend. Once while camping, Steve went to the creek to get some water. He ran back up to the campsite nearly scared to death. He claimed he had seen dwarfs down by the creek. He was so frightened that he had thrown the water buckets down and refused to go back and get them. Dewayne eventually walked to the creek bank, retrieved the buckets, and got fresh water.

On another occasion, while camping in the same place, Dewayne and Steve set up two small bright orange tents with the doors facing each other. In the center, they set up firewood. With their campsite ready for the night, they decided to run to Pennington Gap, Virginia, to get a pizza. They were gone about an hour. When they returned to their campsite, their tents were gone. Now without tents, Dewayne and Steve had to find another shelter. They decided to go to a nearby rock shelter where they had also spent many nights. It was safe and warm. That night, there came a violent storm. There were gusts of wind that the two small tents could have never withstood. Perhaps the little people knew that a storm was coming and that the tents were not safe. Despite searching nearly all of the next day, Dewayne and Steve never found their bright orange tents.

One day, a school friend of mine and I were having lunch together in the school cafeteria. He told me not to think that he was crazy, but he saw little people. He said that tiny people walked around outside his house at night and sometimes, they would even come inside his home. When they came inside, they would walk in a single file line. He often awoke and saw them walking down the hall outside his room. Sometimes, they would come in his room. He also said that his mother and brother had seen the little people many times. He told me that his mother was a Christian and never lied, and that she would tell me the same thing.

I assured him that I believed him, but that evening I got a phone call and it was my friend. His mother was with him and she got on the phone. She told me about her experiences with the little people. She said that she had told her children to act as if they do not see the little people and if they were in bed, to act asleep when the little people arrived.

After he was sure I believed him, my friend often spoke of the little people and he told me that they were exactly like normal people, just miniature. In fact, everything he ever told me fits the description of the Aniyvwi Tsunsdi.

Fifty or sixty years ago, a man from Chicago, Illinois, came to Straight Creek. I do not know who he was or why he came to Kentucky. According to my mother and grandparents, one summer day, he came down out of Pine Mountain behind my grandparents' house.

He and my grandfather began talking and the man told Papaw that, while he was in the woods, he came across four beautiful stones. He laid them down just for a moment and when he turned around to pick them up, they were gone. He told about searching for them, and how they seemed to just disappear into thin air. He said he must return to Chicago, but was coming back the next summer to search once again for the stones. He asked Papaw if he would look for the stones during the rest of the year and Papaw told him that he would keep an eye out for them. The man told Papaw that if he found them, he would give Papaw two of the stones and none of their children and grandchildren would ever have to work.

The man left and Papaw really never thought he would ever see him again, but the very next summer, the man returned and asked Papaw if he had found the stones. Papaw told him that he hadn't and the man began searching again. The man returned every summer for years and searched for the lost stones. One year, he didn't show up and never came back. No one knows what happened to him, but he never found the stones. He described the stones as being clear, so I am assuming he thought they were diamonds. I don't know what they were, but I am sure he didn't ask the Aniyvwi Tsunsdi if he could have them and I think they were the tricksters who took his stones.

Elusive Creatures Of Pine Mountain

Until recently, according to the Kentucky Department of Fish and Wildlife, the only wild cat that resides in the entire state of Kentucky is the bobcat, also known as the Kentucky Wildcat. These felines grow to the size of a small-to-medium sized dog and are rather harmless and shy. I do not know if panthers were released in this area, but they have definitely made a "comeback" to the mountains.

All my life, I have heard tales of huge panthers that dwell in the mountains and forests of southeastern Kentucky. The first person I ever heard speak of these creatures was my grandfather, Isaiah Saylor. He was born in 1913. He would tell of being a young boy and hearing panthers (he pronounced it "painters") growling and roaring in the mountains of Leslie County. He described the cry of a bobcat as being comparable to a woman or child screaming. He said the panther's call was much more frightening and ferocious sounding. He could recall hearing them outside his house at night as a child.

According to my grandfather, there were such large cracks in his house, that when it snowed during the night, he would awake with snow all over his bed. He could hear the night sounds just as if he were outside. He could see out of the cracks in the walls and sometimes, he saw the huge cats quietly roaming around his yard hoping to find a chicken off its roost.

About 15 years ago, a man who lives in Beverly, Kentucky in Bell County, said a panther crept up behind him while he was hunting in broad daylight. Several years ago, I spoke with a young man from northern Kentucky who made weekend trips to Wayne County to try to document that panthers do live in Kentucky. Apparently, this young man was exploring a cave and when he exited, came face to face with a gigantic black panther.

He was very curious about the cat and contacted the Department of Fish and Wildlife to get some information about the animal. He was quickly informed that these cats do not exist in Kentucky. He then decided to dedicate every weekend of his life to prove them wrong.

A year ago, I heard talk of a black panther being spotted in the Cumberland area of Harlan County and just recently, to my surprise, I received an email containing photographs of a black panther that was in a backyard near Pineville, Kentucky, in Bell County. Proof at last! All these sightings and encounters were supposedly when these creatures did not live in southeastern Kentucky. Now there are audio recordings of them and frequent sightings.

It is unbelievable that this majestic creature that has made the mountains its home for hundreds of years was given the status of "nonexistent" due to the lack of documentation despite many eyewitness accounts. I never doubted the existence of the panther. I still remember hearing phrases like "It's untelling what is in these mountains" and "We haven't found everything that roams around these woods." I learned very early in life that the mountains hold many mysteries yet to be discovered. The recent panther photographs made me wonder, "What are in these mountains that we do not know about?" I began remembering stories that I hadn't thought of in years.

On the Harlan County/ Bell County line is a small community called Pathfork. In the mid-eighties, when I was in high school, I had many friends from the Pathfork area. I now realize that we were all related. Pathfork is a very secluded community nestled back in a hollow. My friends from Pathfork would often come to school with very intriguing accounts of unusual happenings that occurred in their neighborhood. A lot of the events centered around a strange creature that they claimed lived in the woods around their farms and homes. They claimed to hear it often and occasionally, would be chased and frightened by it. They also said it killed livestock and pets.

In Pathfork, there was a big old barn that was a gathering place of some local teenagers. The barn had a hayloft and that was where they congregated on the weekends.

The teenagers would play music and socialize until very late at night. On one particular Saturday night, the volume of their stereo began fluctuating. It would be too loud one moment and the next, it would be barely audible. It was agreed by all that the batteries were probably getting old.

Finally, the stereo began turning off and on and once more, this was contributed to the batteries. During the times that the stereo was off, the kids began hearing something outside the barn. A couple of the boys quickly grabbed the old wooden ladder and pulled it up with them. They turned off the stereo to listen and they could hear something circling the old barn. One of them called out, thinking another friend may have arrived, but there was no response. They could hear deep "grunt-like" breathing. All of them knew what it was. They had grown up with the knowledge that something inhuman lurked among them.

Quickly, they turned out their lanterns and went to the large opening in the hayloft. They looked down and there, in the moonlight, was a large figure. It seemed as if it were trying to think of a way to get up to the hayloft. It was pacing and appeared to be concentrating very hard. It was huge, but in the dark, it was hard to see what it really looked like. Everyone remained silent and some were now scanning the loft for makeshift weapons. Down below, the creature still paced and circled the barnyard.

After awhile, the creature slowly crept into the woods. Everyone listened as branches and saplings cracked under its feet. Suddenly, it began to let out loud wails. Some of the teenagers had heard these wails before, but usually when they were safe in their homes.

It sounded part human and part animal. It sounded angry. Like many times before, it wailed in one place and then a second later, it would wail in what seemed to be miles away from where it just was. It was still circling them only now the circle was much bigger. No one had any intention of leaving the loft or trying to go home. They stayed the entire night in the barn and didn't leave until late Sunday morning. The teenagers who had past encounters with the creature all agreed this time was different. This was the first time they felt as if they were its prey. It was obvious that it had been stalking them and had become quite angry when it failed to get to them.

Many residents of Pathfork claim to have heard the creature, but few can say that they have seen it. One boy, who was in the barn that night, had gotten a much better view of the creature a while before that. One morning just at daybreak, he heard his dogs barking and growling. He got up to see what was wrong. He looked out his kitchen window and there it was in his barnyard. It was huge, probably seven or eight feet tall. It was holding a goat it had just killed, and strangely enough, it resembled a goat itself. It seemed to be part human, part goat.

The boy watched the creature until it turned and ran into the woods. Most people say that you can hear it late at night making its strange wailing sound. Many say it only does that when it's hungry. Others have heard it while they were in the mountains hunting. They say that you can hear it moving through the trees and you can hear its heavy feet pounding the ground.

On the other side of Pine Mountain is the small community where I grew up called Straight Creek. The Straight Creek community has its own tales of a large creature that dwells in the mountains.

My cousin, Bonnie, told me one of these tales when I was about eleven years old. When Bonnie was a child, around 1960, she and her sister, Phyllis, liked to go up into Pine Mountain behind their house and play at an old moonshine still that had been abandoned for years. One day, as they were playing, they began to hear something in the woods around them. They could hear something slowly moving as if it were trying to be very quiet.

This concerned the two girls and they decided to start toward home. As they walked down the mountain, they could hear something behind them. When they would turn around to see what it was, nothing was there. The girls were now frightened and they began to run down the mountain.

As soon as they began running, whatever was following them began running, too. They could hear heavy feet hitting the ground. This terrified the girls and they began screaming loudly as they ran wildly. Their neighbor, Dan Cooper, heard the girls screaming and he ran out of his house to see what was wrong. As the girls ran into the clearing, Dan said that he saw nothing chasing them. Bonnie said that, as soon as they ran into the field at Dan's house, whatever had been chasing them stopped and ran back up into Pine Mountain.

These stories about the unknown that dwell in the mountains are my favorites. I have heard others about people being followed, chased, grabbed, and basically scared senseless by things that don't fit into the animal category. I have heard about people finding huge footprints on their porches and in one instance, on their porch ceiling. I recall people telling about having feed and flour sacks torn into and in the spilled flour or feed, they found large footprints. I have even heard about someone waking in the middle of the night to find a grotesque face peering into the window from outside. Will we ever have evidence of these creatures or will they remain a legend? Only time will tell.

Panther in Bell Co., KY
2006, photos courtesy of Sheila Key

As a teenager, I had some very close friends from Pathfork, Kentucky. We would talk on the phone, go places, and on Friday nights after football games, they would come to my house. We would sit in my driveway in a big circle and I would hear some of the scariest stories I have ever heard in my life. My friends are mentioned several times in this book, but because I have not been in contact with them for years, I will not use their names. This story is dedicated to them and their wonderful stories.

The Haunted House

Some say the entire community of Pathfork, Kentucky was built on a burial ground and because of this, the whole community is haunted.

There was a house so haunted in Pathfork, no one would live in it. It had been empty for years. Legend had it, if you knocked on the front door, someone or something would open it. Everyone had always been too scared to attempt this, so this was a story passed down to kids by their parents who claimed to have knocked on the door years before and had it answered by something unseen.

One day, two boys claimed to have knocked on the door and that it opened. They said that they immediately ran away when it began creaking open. The two brothers they told this story to came up with a "great" idea. The brothers told the boys that, if they went back that night and knocked on the door again, they would be in the back looking through a window to see what answered the door. The boys agreed and they met late that night in front of the house.

The two friends went to the front of the house, while the brothers sneaked to the back. The brothers were looking through a large window and could see the living room, the kitchen, and even a small bedroom. The boys in front could only see in the living room. The house was an old farmhouse and quite big. The boys began knocking on the old door. The brothers heard them and began to watch intently.

Suddenly, something arose from an old cot in the small bedroom. It stood up and began floating through the house toward the front door. The brothers began quietly trying to tell the boys in front to stop knocking. When they realized that they couldn't be heard without yelling, they ran around to the front of the house and told the boys to run. All four of them went running down the road. As they were running home, they could hear the old door creaking open.

Buried Alive

Long ago in the mountains, when someone died, the family built a coffin, had the visitation at their home or church, and then, finally, had a burial at a family cemetery without the aid of a mortician, funeral director, or funeral home. This was common practice until the late 1950s. The visitation was called a "wake." I have now learned that it was called a wake because it was a waiting period between death and burial to see if the dead really were dead or if they "wake" up. Someone had to be with the body at all times and for some reason, you had to keep cats away from the corpse. People would take turns sitting with the corpse until burial.

About 55 years ago, a young woman that lived on Straight Creek seemed to die. She was totally unresponsive. Her breathing was so shallow and her heart rate so weak, that she was assumed dead. She was not dead. She was more than likely in a coma. The wake was held at the girl's home and she was placed in a rough pine coffin in the living room. My grandmother, Susie, went to the wake and took her turn sitting up with the assumed corpse. My mother, who was a young child at the time, accompanied her mother and also sat up with the corpse. My mother says that, the entire time that she was there, beads of perspiration would pop out on the girl's forehead. Not realizing that the dead don't perspire, her family members would get a handkerchief and gently blot her forehead dry. That night while my mother and grandmother were sitting up with her, she continued to perspire. They, too, simply grabbed a cloth and dried her off.

The next morning, the young girl was buried - alive. I often wondered if she ever woke up. I can think of few things worse than awaking in a buried casket. There are many cases of people being buried alive before the practice of embalming. Severely ill people can appear dead to those who have no medical training. I hope this young girl did not awake. I hope she died peacefully.

The Abyss

Growing up, I often heard my family talk about a bottomless pit that was supposedly about half-way up Pine Mountain. I do not know the exact location of it, but it seems to be on the Straight Creek side of the mountain, near the trail that used to go across to Wallins Creek.

According to my family, the bottomless pit was about six feet in diameter and very difficult to see. It looked like a common sinkhole and, with a fallen tree or bush over it, was completely camouflaged, especially in autumn with fallen leaves everywhere.

In the 1940s, some farmers were moving their cattle from Straight Creek to Wallins Creek. The farmers were not aware of the pit, and one of the cows strayed off of the path and fell into it. The farmers claimed that they listened for a very long time and never heard the cow hit the bottom.

There are many tales similar to this regarding the bottomless pit. My great-grandmother, Matilda Belcher Saylor, was on her way across Pine Mountain with her two grandchildren, James and Ellie. They stopped to rest for a while and have a snack. Matilda found a cool shady spot to sit and eat. All at once, her leg dropped and she realized she was sitting on the edge of the pit. She had heard of the pit before, but never knew where it was. She cautiously backed away and moved her grandchildren to a safer location. Curious, she began to drop things into it. She started out with small rocks and then progressed to larger things. At last, she dragged a log as heavy as she could move and heaved it into the pit. She claimed she never heard any of the items hit the bottom.

Some young men decided to attempt to find the bottom of the bottomless pit. Several of them got together and found the longest ropes they could. They tied them all together and tied one end around the waist of one of the men. They began lowering him in and sent him deeper and deeper.

It wasn't long before all of their rope was used up. The young man could see by a lantern he was holding. He said that even hundreds of feet deep, no end was in sight. He, like many others before, dropped an object and like all the rest, claimed to never have heard it hit the bottom.

There is a fire tower on the top of Pine Mountain and, as a child, my mom and her friends loved to visit the tower and climb to the top. Whenever she would go, she always feared walking into the pit and carefully watched her every step.

I do believe there is a huge pit in Pine Mountain. I doubt it is bottomless, though it may appear to be due to its depth. With years of debris falling on it, it is probably no longer visible. Hunters and hikers probably walk on it without realizing it; not realizing they are walking on the dreaded bottomless pit.

Bonnie Saylor had lots of great stories. Her name is mentioned several times in this book. She and I spent a lot of time together when I was growing up and some of my fondest memories are staying with her and my Uncle Lonnie.

The House At Stony Fork

Electricity came late to the mountains and in the remote area of Stony Fork in Harlan County and some parts of Bell and Leslie Counties, it came even later. Most houses were built before the days of electricity, so when it was finally available, the old farmhouses were wired very primitively. In some houses, wires weren't inside the walls. They were exposed and dangling here and there. In the more technically advanced homes, light bulbs would be stuck out of the ceilings with a small chain for pulling it "on" or "off." Most of the houses I recall didn't have chains. Light bulbs would have to be twisted on or off and there would be "hot pads" lying around on most every table, dresser, and nightstand for turning off lights when the bulbs were very hot. In the mid-1970s, my cousin, Bonnie, moved into a house that was wired like this.

Bonnie Caldwell's mother, Minnie Mosley Caldwell, and my maternal grandmother, Mossie Mosley Saylor, were sisters. Bonnie married one of my dad's younger brothers, Lonnie Saylor, so she is also my aunt. Bonnie and my Uncle Lonnie moved into an old house at Stony Fork, Kentucky, near Bell County. Straight Creek turns into Stony Fork about ten miles down the creek. I don't know when Straight Creek officially turns into Stony Fork, but the old house Bonnie and Lonnie moved into was definitely at Stony Fork. I remember the house well and I thought it was very cozy and pleasant. I had visited the home when my dad's cousin, Wilke, lived in it. One of the things I remember was that the refrigerator, and possibly the washer and dryer, was on the back porch. The house was built before either of these things existed, so the kitchen was not designed for large appliances.

Bonnie was the secretary at Green Hills Elementary School where I was a student. Lonnie worked at night in the coal mines. Bonnie and our other cousin, June, decided to help with the Green Hills cheerleaders. Because of this, Bonnie attended all of the school's basketball games. Bonnie arrived home from ballgames after Lonnie had already gone to work. On this night, Bonnie got home about 9:00 pm. It was late autumn and had been dark for quite a while.

Bonnie got out of her car, walked up on the small front porch, and began unlocking the front door. She turned the knob and began pushing it open, but to her surprise, the door that normally swung open with ease seemed stuck. After pushing on it a few minutes, her eyes had adjusted to the dark and she could see that the door was open a couple of inches, but would open no more. She pushed with all her might and got it open about six inches. Suddenly, it shut again with a forceful slam. If she didn't know better, she would have thought someone was in the house pushing against the other side of the door. Now that the door was completely shut, Bonnie once again turned the knob and pushed on the door. This time it opened easily.

Although a bit disturbed by the problem with the door, Bonnie knew that old houses settle during the cooler months. Now that she was inside, she simply began doing what she did every night that she got home after dark. She opened the door wide to let in the moonlight and began slowly walking to the center of the dark living room. Bonnie had done this so much that, even in the dark, she could walk straight to the light. She reached up and began twisting the bulb. When she did this, the room filled with light. The second the room was lit, the front door slammed shut so violently that the windows shook. As soon as the door slammed shut, the light went out.

Needless to say, Bonnie panicked and began to run in the now completely dark house. She ran into walls, but finally managed to find her way to the tiny bathroom in the back of the house. She quickly closed the bathroom door and locked it. Once she felt safer, she reached up toward the ceiling for the light bulb. When she found it, she gave it a twist, but the light didn't come on. She unscrewed it all the way out and then back in again, but still, the light would not come on. Not knowing what to do, she stood there silently, her heart racing. She could hear something in the house. It was footsteps walking on the old linoleum floor. The steps were slow and steady. It sounded like they were in the kitchen.

Now desperate to get out of the house, Bonnie unlocked the small bathroom window, stuck her head out, and looked down. She had never noticed how high the back of the house was. The window was 12 to 14 feet high, and she would probably break a leg or ankle if she attempted to jump out of it.

The sounds from kitchen got louder and now, she was hearing what seemed to be furniture being scooted around. With that, Bonnie decided to take her chances. She swung her legs out of the window and held on to the sill with her hands. When she was hanging and had stopped swinging, she let go. Her feet hit the ground and a stabbing pain went through one of her legs. She fell backward as soon as she hit and went rolling down the sloping yard. Despite the fact that she sprained her ankle, she jumped to her feet and ran down the road to the nearest neighbor's house. Unfortunately, she had laid her car keys down on a table as soon as she entered the house.

When she told the neighbors about what had happened, the man of the house got his gun, went to his truck, and drove to Bonnie's house. After about ten minutes, he returned and said that everything was fine. He told Bonnie that the front door was wide open and every light in the house worked just fine. He then drove her home.

Bonnie and Lonnie didn't live in that house much longer, but for the short time they did, nothing like that ever happened again. There were never any problems with the front door sticking or the electricity going out.

The Curse

My grandmother's mother was Sarah Belcher Mosley. Sarah's mother was Alabama Gross and her father was Dan Belcher. Sarah died when I was ten years old, but I remember her quite well. Sarah lived in a little trailer on Straight Creek, set off the road a bit, with a huge garden in front. I loved to visit her and I loved her trailer. I also loved her gold tooth. After my great grandfather, Harrison Mosley, passed away, Sarah briefly wed a man by the name of Adron Sparks. Adron soon died, too. I never knew his name until recently. I only knew him as "Mamaw's Old Man."

Mamaw did what many people in the area did. After her little farmhouse got too old and run down, instead of fixing it, she chose to buy a trailer and set it on the property with the existing house. My cousin, Bonnie, who we now know was not thrilled with her house at Stony Fork, found the little old farmhouse very appealing. She and my Uncle Lonnie began working on the house and as soon as it was livable, they moved in. I spent many nights with Bonnie in that little house. I can remember everything about it. It had a cupboard with a built in flour sifter and a pot belly stove.

After "Mamaw's Old Man" died, Mamaw lived by herself. She loved company, so her grandchildren and great-grandchildren would take time about staying with her. I stayed with Bonnie a lot and my cousin, Lora, stayed with Mamaw most of the summer. In the summer, Bonnie and Lora loved to lie out in the sun. They would put blankets in the backyard, lie on them, and play the radio all day long. I hated sun bathing, so Lora and I would trade during the day. She would visit Bonnie while I stayed with Mamaw.

As soon as Lora arrived at Bonnie's, I would head down the little gravel path to Mamaw's trailer. She would be sitting on the porch and would smile a great big smile when she saw me trotting down the path. Mamaw smiled a lot and when I remember her, I always remember her sweet smile. I was only about seven or eight years old at the time and as soon as I would arrive, I would do things for her. I would take her clothes from the clothes line and fold them. I would sweep the porch and do anything else that needed doing. All the while, Mamaw would be saying, "You're about the smartest youngun' I've ever seen!" To the old people, "smart" meant that you were a hard worker. I loved it when Mamaw bragged on me and that would make me work that much harder. Often, my grandparents would come by and Mamaw would tell her daughter, Susie, how "smart" I was. Susie would always agree and tell of the things that I had done for her at her house.

One summer evening, after I had finished all the chores I could possibly think of, Mamaw and I sat on her front porch. She had metal porch furniture and I preferred an old glider that she had setting on the end of the porch. She always preferred an old cane bottom chair that she moved out from the kitchen. We were eating cornbread and milk. For those of you who do not know, cornbread is crumbled in a bowl and it is eaten like cereal with milk poured on top of it. It was not dark, but the sun was down. The dew was falling and crickets began chirping. Fireflies sparkled in the huge field and garden in front of her house. "Tell me a ghost story, Mamaw," I said.

Mamaw thought for a moment. She said that she didn't know if it was a ghost story, but a long time ago, two women from Philip's Fork got in a fight. Everybody always said that one of the women was a witch. After the fight, that woman seemed to put a curse on the other. Bad things started happening to the other woman, and from that day on, her milk cow would no longer give milk. It only gave blood. Mamaw said that the cow lived a long time and nothing was wrong with it, but whenever someone tried to milk it, all that would be in the bucket was pure blood. She said that everyone saw the cow give blood and after that, no one ever wanted to get in a fight with the old witch.

A couple years later, Mamaw's final days were spent at my grandmother's house. I stayed there most of the time, too. Up until the very end, she always smiled and told me and everyone else how "smart" I was. When Mamaw died, I missed her very much. I feel so fortunate to have had the opportunity to have spent time with her and hear her wonderful tales of days gone by.

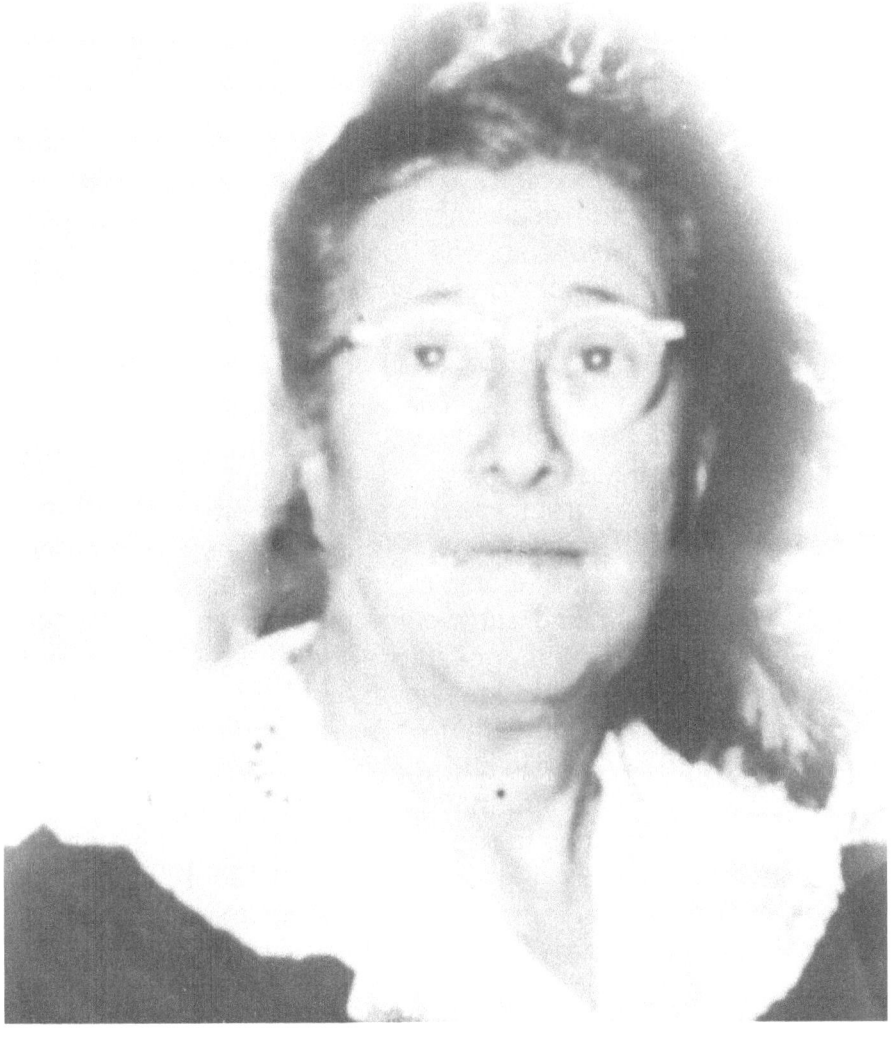

Sarah Belcher Mosley

Straight Creek

Straight Creek is officially called the Straight Creek of the Cumberland River. It is large for a creek and pretty straight, I guess. Supposedly, at one point in time, things rolled out of the creek.

I can barely remember this story, but I asked my mom about it and she, too, remembers people talking of this event. From what we both can recall, this was not a one-time occurrence. People began witnessing logs, rocks, and even boulders roll out of the creek and onto dry land. The things that would come rolling out of the creek would not stop when they rolled upon the creek bank. They would continue to roll until they hit something that would stop them.

My grandmother said that without warning, huge logs and rocks would suddenly emerge from Straight Creek and roll out of the water with great speed and force. She claimed to have seen this with her own eyes. I remember her saying that you had to be very careful not to get run over by these things. Whatever came rolling out, would only stop when it crashed into the side of the mountain or into a large tree or rock. My mom recalls my grandmother saying that, at times, she could hear things rolling out of Straight Creek and crashing into the mountainside even while she was in her house.

I have very little information on this unusual event. I had forgotten about things rolling out of the creek until the other day. I always had a mental image of what I thought this might have looked like and that image popped into my mind. I quickly called my mother and she verified that this was not a figment of my imagination. People often told this story and claimed it was the truth.

Frank Branch

My paternal great-grandmother was Matilda Belcher Saylor. Matilda was known as "Little Mammie." She lived in a hollow that everyone calls Frank Branch. At one time, there were several families living there, but by the late 1940s, she was the only resident of Frank Branch. Her son, my grandfather, Isaiah, lived at the mouth of the hollow and was her nearest neighbor. Matilda lived alone and more isolated than most people today could ever imagine. She had no telephone or any way to communicate with others. She had no vehicle or horse and her only way to travel was by foot.

Matilda lived this way for many years and did not seem to be bothered or frightened by her isolation. My grandfather checked on her often and her grandchildren stayed with her quite a bit. Matilda loved to tell stories and according to her grandchildren, would tell some of the scariest stories ever told, all the while insisting each and every one of them were true.

Matilda's stories seem to be lost forever. All that remain are fragments of memories of children of long ago. One story seems to have survived, strangely enough, remembered by a granddaughter who should be too young to remember. My Aunt Loretta remembers Matilda telling about the ghosts of a woman and her baby that haunted Frank Branch. She would see the woman with her baby walk by her tiny house. Sometimes at night, lying in bed alone, she could hear the pitiful cries of the tiny baby.

Years before, a woman was walking out of Frank Branch at night with her infant. She slipped and both she and her baby rolled down a steep hill. The woman hit her head on a rock and her infant rolled into the branch. Both were found dead the next morning.

Matilda never seemed to fear the woman and baby, but rather, pitied them. She saw the ghosts often and grew so accustomed to them that sometimes she would forget that they were ghosts and assume they were her neighbors of long ago.

Matilda Belcher Saylor

Ouija Boards

I can honestly say I have never used an Ouija Board, although I once watched people make an unsuccessful attempt to use one. The only time I ever saw one was in high school when a couple of girls in the locker room were asking it questions, but nothing happened. I had heard stories about Ouija Boards, so I was reluctant to be in the same room with one, but my curiosity got the best of me.

I find it curious that Ouija Boards are located in the toy department of most stores. They are alongside Monopoly, Twister, Life, and other board games. The Ouija Board, however, is not your typical board game. Supposedly, it is a portal for the spirit world to communicate with our world.

I was warned many times throughout my childhood to avoid the boards at all cost and to never touch one. I was also told that the spirits communicating with you pretend to be "good" when, in fact, they are not. The following are stories that I have heard about Ouija Boards.

The first time I ever heard of Ouija Boards was in 1980 when my friend got one for Christmas. Her mother, like a lot of other parents, assumed it was a game. My friend claimed to successfully use the board and said it knew answers to questions that only she could know. She also claimed it had a personality of its own and that it did not like some of her cousins who used it with her. She did not have the board long until an aunt, who was visiting, told her mother to immediately remove it from the house. Her aunt said that it was evil and told my friend's mother never to burn one or the evil spirit will be left out wandering around. The Ouija Board was placed in the barn and never gotten out again.

I told my cousin, Bonnie, about the Ouija Board, and she said that she had a very disturbing experience with one herself while attending college. Two girls in her dormitory at Cumberland

College, now University of the Cumberlands, in Williamsburg, Kentucky, had an Ouija Board.

Bonnie did not know what one was, so she began asking it questions. She was goofing off and asked it when she would die. The Ouija Board told her that she would die on an April 1 and that a cabinet would fall on her, killing her. Thankfully, that has not happened and probably never will, but every April 1 that must cross her mind. She also said that one night, after using the board, the girls who owned it awoke to find their room had been ransacked and the door was still locked from the inside. After that, they got rid of the Ouija Board.

When I was a freshman in high school, one of my teachers told our class to never play with an Ouija Board. She said that she had gotten one as a child and soon, strange things began happening in her house. Her mother blamed it on the board and took it out and burned it. My teacher said that, as it was burning, you could see a black figure rising out of the smoke. She and her family could hear it making angry growling noises. She often worried about the evil spirit seeking refuge in her home. She also told us never to burn one and to just leave them alone.

One of Darlene Steele's childhood friends, Debbie, once played with an Ouija Board. She had been at a slumber party where one was. She and the other girls began to play with it. Debbie told Darlene that she asked it when she would die and claimed the "eye" on the board went to the number nine. She was pleased and told Darlene that she was going to live to be in her 90s. Only a few years later, Debbie tragically died in an accident at the age of 19. When hearing about Debbie's death, Darlene remembered the number "9" on the Ouija Board.

The Lights Of Cumberland Falls

Cumberland Falls is called the Niagara Falls of the south. It is a huge waterfall on the Cumberland River in Whitley County, Kentucky, near the McCreary County border. It is the only waterfall in the world to have a phenomenon called a lunar rainbow or "moonbow." Victoria Falls in Africa used to have a moonbow, but due to forest cultivation, it has too much light to produce one anymore. Moonbows can only be seen during a full moon on clear nights. They look just like a rainbow and are created much the same way. They are much softer in appearance, though.

The Cherokee that dwelled along the Cumberland River near the falls believed it held great powers. They believed that spirits lived in the smoky mist that emanated from the falls. They would put their dead into the river and let them drift over the large waterfall. Legend has it that the bodies never resurfaced and the Cherokee believed that the bodies went straight to the spirit world through the mist of the falls.

Cumberland Falls has been surrounded by legend for hundreds of years. The Cherokee claimed that it was inhabited by spirits, and there have been many accounts of unusual sights and sounds witnessed around the falls.

Many people have accidentally drowned, fallen over the falls, or fallen off of one of the nearby cliffs. The high rails and restricted areas did not exist as recently as twenty years ago, and I can remember, in the mid-1970s, when swimming was permitted only feet from the falls. Fifty years ago, people were allowed to walk under the falls. I have seen photos from 1915 of boats that were right at the fall's mist. Why they weren't taken under, I'll never know.

Many accidental deaths instigated park officials to implement stricter safety standards. Only a couple of years ago, my family was driving across the Cumberland Bridge above the falls when we saw a man dead in the road. He and his friends had been hiking and he had gotten too close to the edge of the cliff located above the highway. It was October, and the leaves had fallen. Wet leaves can be as slick as ice. He was peering over the cliff when he slipped and fell a hundred feet to his death. Our car approached before authorities had gotten there and I'll never forget the shock and devastation on his friends' faces as they stared at their dead companion.

In August of 2006, a ceremony was held at the nearby Yahoo Falls in McCreary County. Many Cherokee descendants attended this special event. My cousin and friend, Gayla, and her husband, Mike, came from Virginia to the ceremony and stayed at the DuPont Lodge at Cumberland Falls State Park. The night after the ceremony, they decided to visit the falls. There was not a full moon and it was very cloudy, so there were not many tourists waiting to catch a glimpse of a moonbow.

As they were at the overlook, they could barely see the falls in the darkness. As she stood there, Gayla began singing a Native song to her ancestors. Suddenly, little red lights began sparkling in the falls. The lights danced and twinkled for several minutes. Gayla and Mike began looking for a possible source for these lights, but they couldn't find one. There were neither car lights nor any other source for these lights. The red lights continued to flicker in the darkness and were as close as twelve feet away from them as the tiny orbs continued to dance above the water. After about five minutes, the little lights disappeared. Then, to their surprise, a larger white light came from the distance and began to circle them. It darted into some trees, came back out again, and then disappeared.

I have heard other accounts of small twinkling lights in the area of Cumberland Falls. Many say it is Cherokee fairies that come out at night to play. Others say it is the spirits of the Cherokee who lived there long ago. Gayla says she thinks it was the spirits of her ancestors coming out to show their approval of the ceremony performed at Yahoo Falls. Some say they have actually seen the lights turn into small human-looking creatures. I do not know what the lights are, but they can be seen at Cumberland Falls and Yahoo Falls. Anyone who has ever been to either of the falls cannot deny they are magical and sacred places.

Cumberland Falls - Whitley Co., Kentucky

This story was contributed by Douglas from Harlan County. Although he currently lives in Harlan County, this happened to him when he was living in Nancy, Kentucky, which is north of Somerset in Pulaski County.

The Racing Demon

It was a strange night. Douglas was going home from the restaurant he owned in Somerset, Kentucky. It was winter, and there were several feet of snow on the ground. A rare winter thunderstorm had blown in. It was pouring rain and lightning was shooting down from the sky. To make the night even more unusual, the thunderstorm was very isolated, and off in the distant night sky, a full moon glowed brightly. Douglas lived in Nancy, Kentucky, which was about ten miles from Somerset. He drove a red Ford Mustang that he often bragged "could fly."

This particular night, he was traveling much slower than he normally did due to the snow and the storm. Within a few minutes of traveling on the lonely highway, he began to hear a sound outside his car. At first, he couldn't figure out what it was and feared something was wrong with his car. After listening for a while, it sounded to Douglas like the gas tank cover was being flipped over and over again. The cover was on the passenger side, and he glanced over his shoulder to try to see back there. He could see something outside his car. It looked as if someone or something was running alongside his vehicle. It appeared to be "playing" with the gas tank cover and was flipping it occasionally to get his attention.

Douglas knew something really odd was going on, so he sped up to get away from whatever was outside his car. When he did, the thing that was playing with the gas tank cover ran up to the passenger side window and looked in at him. What was peering into his window was some sort of monster or demon. He said that it had horns and a grotesque face. It was bipedal, had hooves for feet, and its skin was gray with black stripes running up and down its body. It had claws and fangs and when it opened its mouth, the inside of it was a fiery red.

Douglas stepped on the gas to get away from this horrifying creature. With ease, the demon sped up, too, and continued to run alongside his car. Occasionally, it would drop behind a bit so that it could flip the gas cover again. After it was finished flipping the gas cover, it would once again return to the passenger side window. The red Ford Mustang was hitting speeds of right around 100 miles per hour and the demon seemed to have no trouble running beside it. It never became tired. It kept looking in the window at Douglas and seemed to be taunting him.

As he neared his house, Douglas began to blow the car horn to alert his wife. As soon as his wife, Susan, heard it, she knew something was wrong and ran outside. Right before he reached his house, the thing outside Douglas' car disappeared. Susan never saw it at all. Needless to say, Douglas was absolutely terrified. He ran inside and grabbed a loaded pistol. He stood and watched for the creature to come running down his driveway, but it never did. Finally, he and Susan went inside and he told her about his wild ride home with a racing demon.

The following stories were contributed by Polly Howard. Polly is a first cousin of Butch Steele and a very close friend of Darlene Steele. All of these stories took place in Harlan County.

The Coal Mine

Polly's father was James "Jim" Howard. Jim was a Christian who had studied the Bible and taught Sunday School for many years. Jim was blessed with the gift of interpretation of the scriptures and brought out the meaning of God's Word in such a way that everyone felt blessed to be in his Sunday School class. All left inspired by his knowledge and understanding of the Bible.

Jim, like many others in Harlan County, worked in the coal mines. One night in 1962, he was working with his close friend, Allen Short. The two were in a low section of the mine where no one else was working at the time. After awhile, they decided to take a break and eat, so they both began opening their dinner buckets. They were eating when they both distinctly heard a man's voice say, "Hey boys, come on down here!" They peered down the mine shaft where the voice was coming from, but could see no one.

The two men sat dumbfounded as they knew they were the only miners in the lower section. Once again, they heard the voice, this time more forceful, "Hey boys, come on down here!" The urgency in the voice convinced the miners that they needed to go see what was wrong. Perhaps a miner from another shift had been injured and needed their help.

They began crawling deeper into the mine shaft toward the voice. They had only been crawling a few seconds when a monstrous boulder fell in the exact spot where they had been eating. After exploring that section of the mine completely, the men discovered that they were the only miners there.

Jim told this story until he died. He always said that God had sent an angel to spare the life of him and his close friend that night in the deep dark mine.

The Sign

In 1958, Jim Howard's young son's appendix burst. To make matters worse, it had become gangrenous, so the boy was critically ill. As his son lay in a hospital bed in Harlan, Jim sat on the end of his son's bed and prayed for his recovery. Jim had a lot of faith in the healing power of the Lord, so he prayed knowing that God could touch his sick son's body and heal it completely.

After Jim was finished praying, he looked at his son and there, over the head of his bed, was a sign that said, "Nothing but the blood." In that instance, Jim knew that God was letting him know that his son would be all right. Jim looked up to Heaven to thank God and when he looked back at his son, the sign had changed and this time it said, "Nothing by mouth."

Jim told many the story about God revealing, through a sign, that his precious son would survive. He never ceased to tell all who would listen about the miracle that took place in that hospital room many years before.

The Man In The Dark

In 1933, Helen Howard, Polly's mother, was ten years old. She lived at Cain Mill Branch in Kenvir, Kentucky. Like most homes in the mountains at that time, Helen's house did not have indoor plumbing. There was a small outhouse located a short distance from the house. One night, Helen awoke and needed to go to the outhouse. She was careful not to wake anyone and slipped out the front door. It was easy to see in the dark because there was a full moon.

Helen made her way back to her house and quietly walked up the steps to her porch. She opened the door and there, in her house standing in the moonlight, Helen could clearly see a man in a black suit and white shirt. This frightened Helen because she did not know this man. He began to walk toward her and then vanished. Two days later, Helen's eighteen-year-old brother was killed when a shotgun barrel exploded while he was holding it. Helen always wondered if the strange man was somehow trying to warn her of her brother's death.

Coal Bin Camp

In the late 1950s, Polly Howard's aunt lived at a place called Coal Bin Camp in Brittain's Creek, Kentucky, located in Harlan County. One night, her aunt's family began to hear what sounded like large rocks pelting their home. The sound was horrifying as it hit the house's tin roof. The sound of rocks raining down on their home lasted for several minutes. When the loud pounding stopped, they cautiously ventured outside to see what kind of damage their house had received. To their surprise, nothing unusual was on the roof or in the yard and the house was perfectly fine. Polly's aunt and her family never came up with any logical explanation of what they heard that night hitting their home.

The road leading into Coal Bin Camp.

This story does not contain shockingly loud sounds or horrifying images, however, the subtlety of these events, to me, makes it all the more scary. In fact, I find this to be one of the scariest stories I have ever heard.

The Strange Sound

In 1945, Polly Howard's grandmother and her family began to hear a low, yet constant, sound in their home. A weird "nnnnnnnnnnnnnnuh" sound could be heard from under furniture, in appliances, and in just about every part of the house. Stranger still, it didn't remain in one place very long. It moved about traveling from one place to another.

Talk of this unexplained phenomenon spread quickly throughout the region, and people came from near and far to hear this unsettling noise. Everyone wanted to experience this for themselves, and Polly's grandmother allowed anyone who wished to hear it in her home in hopes that someone could explain it. She very much wanted to rid her home of this distressing sound. It had interrupted her family's life and especially their sleep. Their once peaceful home was now filled with this constant annoyance. To make matters worse, the house and the area around it was now a tourist attraction of sorts.

The strange sound wandered through the house and maintained its constant buzz for months, and finally, Polly's grandmother could not take it anymore. Lack of sleep and stress had taken their effect on the whole family. Polly's grandmother laid her head on her Bible and prayed to God to reveal what was making this horrible sound. At that very moment, she heard a voice clearly say, "I am here, but you will never know why I am here. I am not here to hurt you." After that, the noise stopped. The strange sound was never heard again. After months and months of the bothersome noise, Polly's grandmother and her family could once again live in peace.

The Slate Dump

Coal always has another material located with it called slate. Although coal is a very hot, clean-burning material, slate is not. In the mining industry, coal that contains slate is undesirable and not as valuable as "clean coal," which is basically slate-free coal. Miners must separate coal and slate. The slate is usually discarded into large piles referred to as a "slate dump." In these slate dumps, smaller pieces of coal can be found, and many mountain families survived the winter by digging through these dumps and picking out the coal to heat their homes. This was, and still is, common practice in the coal fields of southeastern Kentucky.

In 1935, Polly's mother, Helen, was 12 years old. Helen and her sister were sent to the slate dump to fill a coal bucket with enough coal to heat their home for the night. The girls walked down the hollow where they lived at Kenvir, Kentucky, to the slate dump. Near the slate dump was a large flat rock shaped like a table. The girls always passed this rock on their way to and from the dump. Once they arrived at the slate dump, Helen and her sister began to fill their bucket with small pieces of coal. It was nearly dark when they finished and they knew they should be getting home before nightfall.

As they neared the flat rock once again, they began to hear voices. It sounded like chanting and that the sound "pum pum pum pum pum" was being repeated over and over. The voices were low and monotonous and constantly said this strange word. The sisters considered this to be very unusual, but continued toward their home. As they passed the flat rock, they discovered about six or seven old men with long white beards and long white robes sitting in a circle on the rock. Their arms were reaching to the sky and waving back and forth, all the while chanting, "pum pum pum pum pum pum." This strange sight frightened the girls and they ran home unnoticed by the men. Throughout her life, Helen often wondered who the men were and the significance of the strange word they chanted.

Poker Knob Hill

There is an area of Kenvir, Kentucky, in the Clover Fork area of Harlan County where strange phenomena is supposed to occur. Most of the occurrences are in and around a place in Kenvir called Poker Knob Hill at Cain Mill Branch. It is said that, in this area, a baby can be heard crying from an old rock wall. Although many have searched, no one can ever find a baby on or around the rock wall. Locals of Kenvir claim that the crying baby has been heard for many years.

In the 1930s, men would congregate on Poker Knob Hill, build a huge bonfire, and play poker until the wee hours of the morning, thus the name "Poker Knob Hill."

Polly's grandfather, Gilbert, as well as most of the local men at one time or another, enjoyed playing cards on Poker Knob Hill. On one night, Gilbert and several other local men sat playing cards when a man no one recognized walked up and eagerly joined in the game. The stranger was dressed quite oddly, wearing an old worn-out black hat and tattered black suit. Odder still, he had long pointy fingernails. The stranger kept his head down throughout the night and did not look up until he had been beaten at poker so badly that he was broke and ready to leave. Upon his departure, the stranger finally showed his face to the local men, revealing fiery red eyes. Gilbert said that as the quiet stranger with red eyes and long fingernails got up to leave, he looked as if he had come from the very depths of Hell. The men looked on in shock as the stranger slowly turned and walked down the hill. No one ever knew where this man came from and he was never seen again.

Another night while playing cards on Poker Knob Hill, Gilbert said that he saw a women in a long blue dress float down a hill and pass through a barbed wire fence. She then floated to a cemetery where she disappeared. The cemetery is located very near the rock wall where the baby is said to be heard.

Many years later in the 1960s, Polly's uncle was driving on Highway 215 at Kenvir in the very early morning hours. There had been heavy rain that night and all the ditches were filled with water. He was just approaching a road that led to the location where a hospital once stood years ago when he noticed a woman wearing a white hospital gown floating across the rain-filled ditch. She floated into the road right in front of him and just as he prepared to slam on his breaks, she disappeared, leaving Polly's uncle bewildered at what he had just seen.

Poker Knob Hill

The next two stories are about sightings around the Black Mountain area of Harlan County.

The Headless Horse And Its Headless Owner

It has been said that, for many years, a headless horse and its headless owner can be seen in the Black Mountain, Kentucky area. The horse and owner are never seen together and it appears as if they are searching for one another. The headless man is often seen leaned up against an old railroad crossing sign. Many people claim to see one or the other near the old Black Mountain School. Supposedly, decades ago, the man and his horse were struck by a train and both beheaded at the old railroad track at Black Mountain.

Black Mountain, Kentucky

The Sound Of A Drum

There is a place near Black Mountain where the sound of drums can be heard on a hillside. The beating drums have been heard by residents of this area for many years and have been heard as recently as 2004. The drums are not loud, but rather soft and smooth. Listeners, at first, feel the sound above them, but soon realize that it is coming from high on the hillside. No one has ever been able to find a reasonable explanation for the sound of a drum in the dense forest. Many believe it is their Cherokee ancestors coming back to their beloved mountain to reunite in ceremony and dance.

The hillside where the sound of a ghostly drum can be heard.

I do not like urban legends. I find them boring and an insult to real ghost stories. It seems that every area has a haunted highway where someone, usually a girl, will appear in your car and then disappear. Sometimes, a hitchhiker will flag you down and give you directions to a house whereupon arrival, they disappear. You go up to the door and inquire about your traveling companion and a distraught mother tells you that you have just described her son/daughter who was killed on the highway at the exact spot where you picked them up.

This particular story has the "feel" of an urban legend, but with one difference. An urban legend is usually told by someone who was told by someone else, and you can never find anyone that claims they had the experience firsthand. This story is probably the most well known ghost story in Harlan County. There are people who claim to have had this experience, and others that avoid this stretch of highway at certain times of night and certain weather conditions in fear that it will happen to them. It would not be fitting to have a ghost story book highlighting Harlan County without mention of "The Highway 38 Ghost." There are many people today that insist this is true.

The Highway 38 Ghost

Highway 38 runs from the city of Harlan to the Clover Fork area of Harlan County. Highway 38 is not haunted in its entirety. It seems to be haunted only in the area of Coxton, and it is haunted by a woman who met her demise in an area of Coxton called Magazine Hollow. Some say she was found stabbed to death, some say she was hit by a VTC bus, while others say that she was hit by a train.

The Verda Transportation Company was a major form of transportation for Harlan Countians through the years. After a little research, I have discovered that the VTC was in operation as early as 1944. Some of the first reports of a haunting seem to be by VTC bus drivers who looked in their rearview mirrors and saw a young woman in a bus that was previously empty.

Thinking they overlooked her, they would turn around to ask her where she needed dropped off, and then realize that they were alone in the bus. This story also goes back to the days when cars had running boards. Many have reported looking out and seeing a woman holding onto the exterior of their car and standing on these running boards.

Taxi drivers claimed to pick up a girl in Coxton, who was heading to Harlan, and right around the Black Joe, Kentucky area, she disappeared. Others say, that on rainy nights, a young woman will appear in the backseat of your car and ride with you until she finally disappears. It is said that you can see her in your rearview mirror, but if you turn to look, she is not there.

There is one account of this ghostly woman getting into the front passenger's seat. This was told by a man who claimed to have had the experience himself. The woman is said to wear a long flowing dress, and most say that an encounter with this woman will happen on a rainy night around midnight, but some say it can happen at any time. It is said that the woman will only get into a vehicle driven by a man, and some say there simply has to be a male present in the vehicle for her to appear.

About 30 years ago, a man, who is now deceased, was driving through Coxton very late one night when, and to his surprise, a lady appeared in the front seat next to him. This startled the man nearly causing him to wreck his car. Fortunately, he maintained control of the vehicle, and as soon as he left the big curve in Coxton, the woman disappeared. The man told about his frightening experience for many years with such truthfulness that all who heard him believed him.

Another unusual event on this exact stretch of highway happened to Darlene Steele's nephew in 1978. Darlene, her sister-in-law, and all of their children were coming back from Harlan one night after going to the movies at the Margie Grand Theater. They were returning home to Evarts on Highway 38 and were passing through Coxton when Darlene's six-year-old nephew said, "I just saw an angel fly down by our car."

When recently asked if he remembered this event, Darlene's nephew said that he remembered it well. He said that a woman with wings flew by the back of the car and then right by his window. He also said that the women flew outside the car until they reached the Verda community, which is several miles away.

This is not the first group of travelers to see this woman. Other families claim to have been traveling through Coxton when they, too, saw what they believe was the Highway 38 ghost.

I have heard tales of the haunted curve and ghostly woman most of my life. The first time I heard of the ghost was in the mid-1970s as a small child. I heard it again as a teenager in the 1980s and then finally, as an adult. My first encounter with it was the "VTC bus version." Then I heard the "lone traveler with an unwanted passenger in the back" version many years later. This story may have origins as early as the 1920s and 1930s.

Haunted curve of Highway 38. A new road replaced the original.

Magazine Hollow in Coxton, Kentucky.

*The next two stories were graciously contributed by Ray Steele.
I do not consider these ghost stories. Both are amazing stories
of contact with the afterlife.*

The Guardian Angel

Ray Steele had been experiencing "blacking out" episodes for
a couple of years. One day, in January 2006, while walking his
English bulldog near his home, Ray passed out and fell over a
snowy hillside. After about an hour, Ray finally regained
consciousness and with the help of his faithful dog, managed to
climb back up to the road and walk home.

The near tragic event convinced Ray that it was time to see a
doctor. Upon visiting the doctor, it was determined that he was
having cardiac blockage and needed four stints. He was
admitted to St. Joseph Hospital in Lexington, Kentucky, for his
surgery. Ray was going to have three surgeries. The four stints
were going to be put in two at a time. The last surgery was to
see if he had permanent heart damage and to determine if he
needed a pace maker and/or defibrillator.

During the first procedure, Ray refused anesthesia, but
agreed to be given medication to relax him as well as a pain
reliever through an IV. A nurse informed him when the
procedure began and then again when the two needles were
being placed into the arteries. Although the medication in his IV
was to make him drowsy, Ray's nervousness counteracted the
effect, and he was wide awake and becoming very tense.

Ray was watching the doctor and nurses in the operating
room when he noticed a shadowy figure appear. He turned his
head toward the figure and recognized it immediately. It was his
best friend, Michael, wearing the same green military uniform
that he was wearing the last time Ray saw him in December
1970.

Ray's family briefly moved from Evarts, Kentucky, to
Dowagiac, Michigan, in the mid-1960s because his father was
seeking employment at a factory there. Ray and Michael quickly

became best friends. The two were inseparable, and when they were not in school together, they were at each other's houses. They formed a close bond while growing up together and decided that after they graduated from high school, they would enlist in the Army together. After much deliberation, Ray decided not to, but Michael followed through and enlisted. It was very difficult to say goodbye on that cold December day in 1970. Michael was going to Vietnam, and Ray feared it would be the last time he ever saw him.

Two months later on February 2, 1971, only eight weeks after his arrival in Vietnam, Michael was killed in action. His death was devastating to family and friends. The whole community mourned the loss of the young soldier.

Now, Ray lie in an operating room staring in shock at his best friend who was killed thirty five years ago. Michael began to smile and nod his head as if telling Ray that everything was going to be okay. He never spoke, but his presence was reassuring and comforting. Ray wasn't as frightened as he had been when the procedure first began. He was now calm and was certain that Michael had come to tell him that everything was going to be all right. Michael then walked close to the operating table and put his hand on Ray's shoulder. As soon as he did, Michael disappeared. Ray asked one of the nurses if she saw someone else in the room and she said she had not.

Ray fortunately had no permanent heart damage, and he soon made a full recovery. He told his wife, Linda, what had happened to him, and she told him that Michael was his guardian angel. Ray thinks about his experience every day. Seeing his old friend was wonderful and something that will stay with him for the rest of his life.

Going Home

Ray Steele's wife, Linda, passed away on June 14, 2006, in the mid-afternoon at Holston Valley Regional Medical Center in Kingsport, Tennessee. She was buried on Red Bud Hill in Evarts on June 17, 2006, which also happened to be her birthday. Linda was 57 years old when she passed away, and she and Ray had been married 36 years. They had known each other for 48 years, and as children, Linda was a cheerleader for Ray's little league baseball team.

Linda had suffered from diabetes for many years. Through the years battling this disease, she had suffered four heart attacks, kidney failure, and had to have her right leg amputated just below the knee. Several years before the amputation, Linda was confined to a wheelchair. During the course of his wife's illness, Ray stood lovingly by her side caring for her in every way possible.

In the spring of 2006, Linda was admitted to the hospital as she had been many times before, but this time was different. She was more severely ill than she had ever been. Upon her arrival to the hospital, she was immediately placed in the kidney dialysis unit. She was also placed on a breathing machine that was delivering 100% oxygen into her lungs. Ray told the doctors that he did not want any tubes put down her throat. The doctors told him that it would cause more pain and discomfort than it would help anyway.

While Linda was critically ill, family members heard her calling out for her mother who had passed away a few years before. Her voice was slurred and much of what she said was hard to make out, but she would distinctly call out for her mother at times. On her eighth day in the hospital, Linda had 68 pounds of fluid taken from her body, and on the ninth and tenth days, her vital organs began shutting down. Ray asked the doctor to tell him his wife's prognosis. The doctor told him that, as a doctor and friend, he did not feel that Linda would live the rest of the day.

After the conversation with the doctor, Ray and Linda's sister sadly walked to Linda's hospital room. As they were standing at her bedside, she began to mumble. As Linda was trying to tell her sister something, Ray felt something bump up against him and then tug on his shirt. He turned around, fully expecting to see someone behind him, but no one was there. He then began to feel a blast of cold air swirling all around him. This was not a frightening experience for him, just unusual. The swift current of cold air seemed to leap from him and make a path straight to his sister-in-law who stood a few feet away. Ray asked her if she felt it and she said she did. Within seconds, Linda miraculously began breathing on her own. A nurse came in and was amazed at Linda's improved condition. Linda was taken off the breathing machine and given mild oxygen from two small tubes placed in her nose.

For two more weeks, Linda lived happy, alert, and pain free. She was able to fully communicate and speak the entire time. She was able to eat and drink and she had good circulation until the last four hours of her life. During this time, Linda prayed to God and told Him that, if it was His will for her to go home with her family, she was ready to make her Heavenly journey. Linda stayed in good spirits until the very end of her life. She was at peace with whatever the Lord's will was for her. Ray felt a loving warmth envelope him and had not felt any dread since the day Linda began breathing on her own.

Ray and Linda had had a baby named Vickie that died many years ago. Right before Linda passed on, she told Ray that Jesus had told her that He was going to allow her to cross over to the other side and that Vickie would be waiting for her. Linda smiled and told Ray that she and Vickie would be waiting for him when it was his time to cross over. She told Ray that she would get to hold Vickie first, but he would get to when his time came.

Linda spoke until the last minutes of her life. In her final moments, she told Ray and the others at her bedside that her mother, grandmother, Vickie, and Ray's parents were all with her.

Ray and Linda never told one another "goodbye," as it always sounded too final. They always said, "See you later." Linda's very last words were, "See you later, I'm going home."

This story was contributed by Royce Wynn.

Mam

Royce's grandmother was Margaret Thomas. Everyone called her Mam, which was short for Mamaw. Mam was from a community in the Clover Fork area called Dizney. She never lied and wasn't someone who told lots of stories. She was a good Christian woman with much faith in God and was the wife of a minister. Mam had two stories that she told throughout her life and claimed they were absolutely true.

When Mam was a young girl, there were no cars. People in the Dizney area traveled by horse and buggy. At night, these buggies had lanterns that hung on them to help light your way. One night, Mam and her parents were coming home from church. Up ahead of them, they saw the lantern light of another horse and buggy. Mam's father began to steer their buggy over to the side of the road so that the oncoming buggy could pass. Mam watched as the buggy approached. Just as the buggy was passing them, it disappeared into thin air.

Many years later, Mam was still living at Dizney. One day, she looked out of her window and saw her father walking down the road. This would not be unusual except that her father had been dead for many years. She watched as he made his way toward the front of her house. As he approached, she quickly ran to the front door. Now on her front porch, she could no longer see her father. As she was standing there thinking about what she had seen, her front gate slowly creaked open and then slowly shut all by itself.

The original road at Dizney is now a creek bed.

Mam's house and the gate that she saw open by itself. The home is still lived in and owned by her family.

Page 68

The next two stories were contributed by Luada Wynn.

The White Mist

Luada Wynn suffered a massive heart attack in late April of 2006. Doctors at the Baptist Regional Hospital in Lexington, Kentucky, described her heart as having been blown out like a tire. They also told her that it was miraculous that she survived such a cardiovascular event. What was more unusual is that Luada had the heart attack eleven days before she even went to a doctor. She says that she only felt tired and had some pain. It was only on the eleventh day that she felt that something was wrong. When she arrived at the hospital, the large artery in her heart was completely destroyed and her lungs were filled with blood.

As soon as Luada arrived at the Harlan Appalachian Regional Hospital, she was flown by helicopter to Baptist Regional Hospital. On May 12, 2006, she underwent open heart surgery to patch the large hole in her heart. Immediately after her surgery, Luada was placed on a respirator to help her breathe.

She was placed on the respirator from 7:00 am until 2:00 pm, and it was during this time that she heard a man's voice tell her to breathe. As she attempted to breathe, she cried out in pain and found it difficult to take the first breath on her own. She opened her eyes and looked down, but could not see her own body. She found herself in a huge, dark, circular tunnel.

Luada's son, Ronnie, had been killed in a tragic accident at the age of 29. She and Ronnie had always shared a close bond. As she was floating in the tunnel, Luada could feel her son's presence very near. Luada said to her son, "If you can hear Mommy, tell God that she needs help breathing." At that point, a white smoky mist filled the large tunnel. Luada began breathing on her own, and she breathed in the white mist and blew it back out. She could feel Ronnie all around her.

After several breaths of the white mist, Luada saw a flash of light and found herself in the intensive care unit. Luada told her husband, Royce, about being in a large tunnel. Royce told her that he had been with her the whole time, and she never left her bed in ICU.

Vision Of The Coal Mine

In 1980, Luada Wynn had an unusual experience. One evening as she got ready for bed, she began having a vision. In the vision, she was riding in a coal shuttle deep inside a coal mine. She could feel the cold damp darkness all around her. As she rode in the coal shuttle, Luada could see round thick cables hanging from the roof of the mine. Although she could see this vision with her eyes open, when she closed her eyes it became much more vivid. She felt as if part of her was lying in bed and another part of her was in a coal mine.

This frightened Luada, and she told her husband what she was experiencing. Although Luada had never been in a coal mine before, she was describing one with complete accuracy. At one point, Luada saw the number nine etched onto a metal plate. She could see the number nine flashing as she entered another section of the mine.

The vision of the coal mine lasted nearly 45 minutes, and even though it had ended, Luada could not help thinking about it the rest of the night. Luada's brother, Bud, worked in a coal mine, and she was urgent to talk to him about what she had seen. The next morning, she went to her parents' home where she felt that Bud would be and sure enough, he was there. She told her father and brother about what she had seen in her vision. They could not believe how she was describing, in perfect detail, the inside of a mine. Her brother, Bud, said that Luada was describing the coal mine at Yancey, Kentucky, where he worked. The coal company was planning on opening a new section of the mine called Section Number Nine.

Bud worked the third shift, but after Luada's vision he felt apprehensive about going to work that night. He decided never to return to that particular mine again. Sometime later in the Yancey Mine, there was an accident, and a miner was injured in Section Number Nine. Bud feels that Luada's vision saved him from being injured or killed.

Darlene Steele's Stories

The following stories were contributed by Darlene Steele. Darlene was born and raised in the area of Dowagiac, Michigan. While in her mid-teens, she met and married Oscar "Butch" Steele. She moved to Butch's hometown of Evarts, Kentucky, in Harlan County and, with the exception of two years, has lived there ever since. Darlene has three grown children and grandchildren. After her children were raised, Darlene went to college and fulfilled her dream of being a teacher.

Darlene was my son's third, fourth, and fifth grade teacher. Holden had not been in third grade very long when he began coming home with some really great stories. Apparently, Darlene had told the children a story one day, and it wasn't long before they began to beg her to tell them more. Her stories soon became a reward for good behavior or a job well done. Every evening I would ask Holden, "Did Mrs. Steele tell you any good stories today?" Occasionally, the children would talk her into telling them a scary story and those were the ones that interested me the most. The stories Holden brought home were so wonderful that I began to spend time with Darlene and I would ask her to tell me stories. We would sit together on class field trips and would even call each other from time to time.

Then, unfortunately, Holden's tiny school closed and everyone went their separate ways. Darlene Steele was such an influential person in Holden's life that I refused to lose touch with her. We continued to talk on the phone and communicate through letters. Holden also kept in touch with her and would often write her letters and send her recent photographs. To Holden, Mrs. Steele was more than just a teacher. She had become a mother figure and someone he could confide in and rely on. Most children, at least once, become angry with their teachers, but I have never heard Holden say one negative thing about her. In fact, he always came home from school with the utmost praise of her. To me, Darlene became a friend and someone that I loved to talk to and spend time with.

Darlene has such a wonderful rapport with students and parents that she leaves a lasting impression on all who is fortunate enough to know her.

Not long after I began to write this book, Holden said, "You can't possibly write a ghost story book without Mrs. Steele's in it!" I totally agreed, so I asked her if I could write about her stories. She immediately said yes and began to write notes of her own to give to me. These stories were taken from those notes and from frequent meetings where we would get together, and I would get the treat of listening and watching her tell her stories. More than once, I have sat in a crowded Mexican restaurant and found chills running up and down my arms while listening to these stories.

Darlene Steele has a soft smooth voice and is so pleasant to listen to. I could sit all day and listen to her stories. She is totally honest and all of her stories are the truth. She and her family have many experiences with the unexplained.

Darlene is a Christian and does not believe in dabbling with any of the "black arts." As far as she knows, no one in her family has ever practiced witchcraft or black magic of any kind. She does not believe in trying to contact the dead or seeking the help of psychic mediums. Things such as this are firmly against everything she believes in. Her family feels the same way she does. No one in Darlene's family professes to be psychic and they do not have any mental illnesses that might result in hallucinations. She does not know why strange and unusual things happen to her and her family. It seems that Darlene and her family have an ability to see a certain energy that most others cannot. This ability runs in both sides of her family and seems to have for many years.

Not all of these stories took place in Kentucky, but they have Kentucky ties through Darlene. Several other people in the stories have Kentucky connections as well.

Darlene Steele

The Protective Spirits

In 1972, Darlene was pregnant with her second child. She and her husband, Butch, were living with his parents. Only a few months before, Butch's grandmother, Grace, had died. She had been living in that house at the time of her passing. Darlene and Butch were given a back bedroom to stay in. Butch's sister, Luada, and her husband, Royce, were also living there.

One night, Butch had stayed up very late to watch television and went to bed much later than everyone else in the house. He had just gone to bed when he heard a familiar sound. It was the sound of his grandmother's house slippers scooting across the floor. Grace hadn't been able to pick her feet up for years, so she shuffled when she walked, making a very distinct sound. Seconds later, Mamaw Grace walked into the bedroom where Butch was and shuffled past the bed and on to another room. She was wearing her favorite nightgown and bonnet, and long after she had gone, Butch could still smell her. Mamaw Grace always had a sweet smell about her.

Another night, Darlene awoke and needed to use the restroom, so she got up and made her way down the hall. The bathroom door was old and hard to open. She gave it a hard push that made quite a bit of noise. She was returning to her bedroom when she passed by Royce's bedroom and noticed that he was sitting up in bed, looking very pale and acting strangely. She apologized for making so much noise and for waking him.

For several days after that, Darlene noticed Royce was still acting unusual. She assumed he was angry at her for waking him up. A few days after, Luada came to Darlene and told her that she did wake Royce, but he was not angry at all. Apparently, Darlene had entered the bathroom quickly before Royce had even sat up in bed. Royce never saw her enter. What he did see was Mamaw Grace coming out of what used to be her bedroom. She went to the bathroom door and walked through it. When the bathroom door opened, Royce did not expect to see Darlene. He never knew she was in there. He expected to see the apparition of Mamaw Grace again. Darlene always thought that Mamaw Grace's spirit was checking on her to make sure she was all right.

Another similar event happened to Darlene when she was nine years old. She awoke in the middle of the night and needed to use the restroom. She slept with her sister and she climbed over her to get out of bed. She landed on the floor with a pretty loud thumping noise. She went down the hall, went to the bathroom, and then returned to her room.

The next morning, her father told her that she had awakened him. He told her that, as she passed his room, a woman with long black hair was floating in the air behind her. It seems that this was another protective spirit making sure she made it back to bed safely.

Much later in the 1980s, Darlene's son, Butch, Jr., saw a young man standing, staring intensely at the back door. He was wearing a white tee shirt, jeans, brown leather jacket, and red bandana. He never looked away from the door and finally, disappeared. Darlene had not told anyone, but she had heard, on several occasions, noises at the back door and feared someone was trying to break in. She feels that the young man was yet another protective spirit keeping her family safe and watching over them.

The Smoky Figure

This occurrence took place at Darlene's mother and father-in-law's house. It was 1979 and she had taken her sister-in-law, Luada Wynn, to Middlesboro, Kentucky, to see an ear, nose, and throat specialist. This was an all-day trip and they had to wait hours before Luada finally saw the doctor. It was late fall and by the time they left the doctor's office, it was already dark and getting pretty late.

Darlene and her family lived in the Evarts area of Harlan County near Red Bud Hill. This was over an hour's drive from Middlesboro and they did not arrive home until around 10:00 pm. Since it was late, Luada told Darlene to drop her off at her parents' house, and she would call her husband, Royce, to come and get her. This would save several minutes of traveling time for Darlene. She pulled in the driveway and they both got out. Darlene was going in to visit for a moment.

As they got out of the car, they noticed something strange behind the house. It was a dark and smoky figure that was incredibly large, probably about nine feet tall. It was in between the house and a dirt bank that was a few feet from the back of the house. Luada saw it first. She said that it was actually bent over and as they were getting out of the car, it "stood" up. The figure was not that of a human, but had more of a rounded shape to it. This frightened both of the women and they ran into the house. Darlene told her in-laws about what they had seen outside. She refused to go back outside alone. Her father-in-law went outside and turned her car around for her, so she could pull straight out of the driveway. He then walked her out to her car. As she walked to her car, the first thing Darlene noticed was that the large dark figure was still out there, but it had moved quite a bit. It was now near the rabbit cage that was also behind the house. Her father-in-law also saw it. She quickly jumped into her car and drove away.

Not long after Darlene got home, she received a disturbing phone call. Her sister, Cheryl, called from Michigan to tell her that their father was very ill and in the hospital. The doctor had told Cheryl that their father was stable for the time being, so she went home for the night.

Very early the next morning, Darlene received the phone call she had been dreading. Her Aunt Ginny informed her that her father had passed away the night before. He had died about four hours after she had seen the dark figure, and she believes that this was somehow a premonition of his death.

The bank where the smoky figure appeared.

I first heard this story in December of 2003, right after it happened. Darlene and I sat together on a bus in route to Abingdon, Virginia. The entire school was going to Barter Theater to see a Christmas play. Although the play was very good, my favorite part of the trip was sitting with Darlene and listening to this story.

The Blue Light

In November 2003, Darlene went into her son, Zachary's, room, and to her surprise, what appeared to be a blue ball of light was floating about a foot from the right side of his head. Zachary was at his computer, as he often was, and right beside him was this strange-looking ball of light. As Darlene watched, it slowly began to disappear. Zachary was not aware of the ball and Darlene never told him about it.

The next day, Darlene's granddaughter, Ariel, got up first thing in the morning and began to snap photos all over the house. Darlene had just bought a disposable camera and Ariel had decided to put it to use. After she used all the film, she put the camera aside and it was forgotten.

Ariel had been invited to a friend's house. As Darlene prepared to take her, Ariel let out a hysterical scream. Darlene ran to her and the young girl could barely speak. It took Darlene a long time to calm her down. When she finally did, Ariel told her that she had ran into Zachary's room and saw an angel hovering above him. She described it as being blue and glowing, but it had a human form.

In January 2004, Darlene discovered the disposable camera and got it developed. She took it to a one hour photo shop and after the photographs were developed, she went out to her car and looked at them. In a photograph of Zachary, there is a huge blue ball. Darlene took the photograph back into the shop and asked what had happened to it. The film developer told her that nothing had happened during the developing process. He showed her the negative and that the object was present on the photograph before developing.

In June 2006, Darlene visited her family in Michigan. Butch had lived in Michigan and been married before he met Darlene. He and his first wife had a son who had passed away. His son, Byron, was born in 1969. Butch asked Darlene to put flowers on his son's grave while she was there. Darlene told him she would find the prettiest flowers she could. She and her mother went to the cemetery that is located seven miles out of Dowagiac toward Niles, Michigan. She had found some beautiful flowers at a floral shop and knew Butch would be pleased with them. She got a camera and took photos of the grave to show him how nice it looked. When she got the film developed, a strange blue light appears in the photos of Byron's grave.

The Man In The Blue Suit

In 1986, Darlene and her family moved into a house on Red Bud Hill that was over 70 years old. The very day that they moved in, Darlene's daughter, Tammy, was standing at the kitchen sink when suddenly she said, "Mom, I just saw a man wearing a blue suit come through the front door and go in your bedroom." Believing Tammy had just seen a shadow, Darlene walked in her bedroom where her husband, Butch, was and jokingly asked him if a man in a blue suit had walked in there. Butch looked at Darlene and rolled his eyes and it was evident that he saw nothing.

A couple of years later, Darlene's son, Butch, Jr., spent the night and slept on the sofa in the living room. The next morning, he told Darlene that he had seen a man in a blue suit walk through the kitchen.

Around this same time, Darlene's mother visited her from Michigan. She and Darlene were in the kitchen and Darlene was standing at the stove. They were talking and suddenly, her mother's eyes got big. She said that she saw a man in a blue suit walk out of Darlene's bedroom.

After quite a few years of living in the old house, Darlene and Butch tore it down and put a double-wide trailer where it had been. They lived in the trailer while they were building a new home.

In early 2004 while living in the trailer, Darlene's son, Zachary, was visited by the ghosts of a man and woman. One night while lying in bed, he noticed the room suddenly got very cold. He looked up and saw a man and a woman floating a couple of inches above the foot of his bed. The man had dark hair and was wearing a blue suit and tie. The woman had red shoulder-length hair and was wearing a dress. The man said that he and his wife had been killed in a car accident. He told of driving too fast and hitting an oil truck.

The next morning, Darlene awoke to find her granddaughter, Ariel, asleep with a large white Bible resting on her chest. Darlene asked her why she was sleeping with a Bible. Ariel told her that she had heard strange noises in Zachary's room the night before and it had frightened her.

Zachary was convinced he was having a mental breakdown and insisted that he be taken to a psychiatrist. Darlene and Butch tried their best to calm Zachary down, but he was certain that he had lost his mind.

About six months had passed since Zachary's encounter with the two spirits. Darlene and Butch were sitting at the kitchen table. Darlene saw something moving in Zachary's room. A man with dark hair, wearing a blue suit and tie, walked through the doorway. Since Butch did not believe in such things, Darlene did not tell him what was happening. Butch's back was to the man. She continued to watch the man as he walked out of Zachary's room and into the living room. He looked at Darlene and could tell that she could see him. This somehow startled him and he stopped dead in his tracks. He must have thought that no one could see him. Seeming shocked and embarrassed, he quickly disappeared. Darlene had wondered if Zachary had dreamed about the couple in his room, but seeing the man for herself made a believer out of her!

Children Running

In the late 1970s, Darlene and her family moved into a house at Red Bud, Kentucky and lived there for nearly a year. The entire time they lived there, they never experienced anything unusual, that is, while they were inside the house. When they were outside, though, they would hear strange noises coming from inside.

When the family went somewhere and returned home, they could hear what sounded like children running through their house as they approached. The sound of small feet running could be heard loud and clear, but when they opened the front door, all was silent. They didn't have to be gone long or go somewhere far to hear this sound. Even after a quick trip to the store, the running and playing inside the house could be heard. The sounds did not occur when the family was outside or on the porch. They would actually have to go somewhere and return before they'd hear the sounds inside the house. Many times, Darlene would stop and listen before she opened her front door. It sounded like a lively game of hide-and-seek or tag. There were never voices, though, just the sounds of small playful feet.

One night, Darlene and her family went out. Meanwhile, her sister-in-law and cousin dropped by for a visit. As they got out of their car, they realized no one was home. The house was dark and the car was gone. As they turned to leave, they, too, began hearing the sounds inside the house. They walked up to the front door so they could listen closely. They stood and listened in disbelief. In the dark house, they could hear the sound of running. They never thought it was a burglar or an intruder because it didn't sound like that. It sounded like children playing.

The next day, Darlene's sister-in-law and cousin told her about what they heard at her house the night before. Darlene told them that she had heard it many times before. Darlene was never frightened by the sounds she heard inside her house. It just seemed as if the spirits of children were anxious for the family to leave, so they could continue their games of long ago.

Pfieffer Hall was constructed in the early 1940s due to a large increase in the female population of Union College. It opened its doors December 31, 1942. It was named for Mrs. Annie Merner Pfieffer who donated much of her time and money to the school.

Union College

In the school year of 1997-1998, Darlene stayed part time at Pfeiffer Residence Hall at Union College in Barbourville, Kentucky, which is in Knox County. She had eight o'clock classes that were hard to get to from Evarts, Kentucky, on time. In the winter months, it would sometimes be impossible to get there at all. The practical thing to do was stay in one of the dormitories on the nights before the early classes.

One morning at the dormitory, Darlene was heading to her early class. She left her room and walked down the long hallway. She turned a corner and a cleaning lady gasp in fright. Darlene apologized for startling the women. The cleaning lady said that she thought Darlene was the lady who haunted Pfeiffer Hall. She told Darlene that the former supervisor would not go upstairs at night because of something that had frightened her up there. The cleaning lady went on to tell Darlene that she hated to clean Pfeiffer Hall even in the daytime.

It wasn't long before Darlene made friends with the young lady who roomed across from her. She was a nice girl who frequently visited Darlene in her room. On one of her visits, she told Darlene how the administrative building, currently Speed Hall, and Pfeiffer Hall were haunted. She said that both were haunted by the woman whose portrait hangs at the administrative building and students had seen her looking out of the attic windows of that building. Speed Hall was apparently this woman's home at one time. It used to be a private residence. It is also said that this woman died under mysterious circumstances. Darlene then told the young woman all that the cleaning lady had said.

Not long after that, in the fall 1997, Darlene awoke one morning at 5:30 am. It wasn't long before she had to get up, and feeling completely rested, she decided to go ahead and begin preparing for early morning class. She gathered her things and headed to the bathroom down the hall for a shower. She opened her door, went into the hallway, and saw her young friend stepping out of the bathroom.

At the end of the hall, a yellow light suddenly appeared. Both women watched as the light quickly streaked toward them. All at once, the light stopped and in it, you could plainly see the image of a woman. The light then went back in the direction it came from and disappeared. Darlene and the young lady looked at each other in total amazement. They were both speechless and never discussed what happened to them. Darlene didn't want to talk about it because she had to stay in that dormitory if she wanted to get her degree. She tried to not dwell on what she had seen and in spring of 1998, she left the dormitory and never returned.

Pfieffer Hall - Union College, Barbourville, Kentucky

The Faceless Spirit

One spring morning in 1990, Darlene was sitting at her kitchen table paying bills while her son, Zachary, was in the living room watching television. As she sat writing, she noticed something in the corner of her eye. She looked up and saw a figure in the back room. It began to move toward her. She had always heard that fear strengthened evil, so she began to pray to God to give her the strength to sit there and not get up and run. As she continued to pray, the gray figure walked across the kitchen.

The figure was very blurred and distorted. Darlene did not look directly at it. She kept her head down and tried to act as if she were ignoring it. It walked into her daughter's bedroom and sat down on the bed. When it did, Darlene looked in at it. The figure turned to face her. She noticed that it had no face. Where its face should have been was flat, blank, and gray. As it sat there on the bed, Darlene acted as if she were not paying it any mind. She continued to write checks and address envelopes. She could see in the corner of her eye that it would look at the wall and then turn to look at her.

After what seemed like an eternity, the figure stood up again and began to walk back into the kitchen. Darlene once again began to pray and did not look up at it. This time, it was coming right at her. She began to pray harder than she ever had. It passed right by her and began to walk back into the room it came from. As it did this, Darlene looked up at it. Although it was distorted, it had the form of a man. It had no feet, but it had legs and was walking without touching the ground. She never could sense whether it was good or evil, but luckily, she never saw it again.

Eleven years later, in 2001, Darlene's son, Zachary, and granddaughter, Rachel, claimed to see a similar being. One night, Zachary decided to sleep in the living room. He awoke in the middle of the night to find a figure with glowing red eyes, wearing a white gown, sitting in the recliner. The figure was holding a black book in one hand and a lit candle inside a votive in the other. The spirit never spoke and silently sat looking at

Zachary. For some reason, Zachary was not afraid of it. Finally, the spirit set the book and candle down on an end table and stood up. It walked over to Zachary and picked him up. It carried him out of the front door and onto the porch. The spirit then pointed to the mountains toward the northeast with its right hand, while still holding Zachary with its left arm. It then carried him into the house and put him back on the sofa. After doing this, it immediately disappeared.

Darlene may have dismissed Zachary's story as just a dream had not it been for her seven-year-old granddaughter, Rachel. Darlene awoke to find Rachel in bed with her and her husband that same morning. Rachel had gone to sleep in Zachary's room. She told Darlene that she had awoke in the middle of the night and saw a strange person in the house. She described this person in much the same way as Zachary had described the figure he encountered. As the spirit turned to walk away, despite her fear, Rachel said she was compelled to follow it as if she had no will of her own. The spirit walked into a spare bedroom. She described it as having a white gown and glowing eyes. She added that it had no feet. The figure stood quietly and turned its head to look up at the northeast mountains. At that point, she no longer felt controlled by it and ran into Darlene's bedroom and got in bed.

Zachary and Rachel were not aware of each other's experiences at the times when they told Darlene. Rachel is now twelve years old and still tells this story without varying in detail from the first time she told it.

In October 2001, Darlene and her family tore down the house and put a double-wide trailer where their house used to be. It was hard for them to get used to a new home placed exactly where their old home had been.

A couple of days after moving in, Darlene, exhausted from the move, decided to take a nap. She hadn't been there long when she heard noises coming from her closet. She assumed that it was mice getting into the duct work. When her husband, Butch, got home from work, Darlene told him about the noises and said that she wanted new ductwork to keep out the rodents.

Butch built houses for a living, so within a day or two he had replaced all the original ductwork with a much sturdier one, which made it much harder for mice to chew. After he was done, Butch told Darlene that he saw no sign of rodents.

About a week later, Ariel, Darlene's granddaughter, was in the same bedroom when she heard a similar sound in the closet. After that, Darlene heard the sounds coming from her closet many times. She soon realized that her closet was in the same place where her son's bedroom used to be, and that was the room where the faceless spirit had emerged years before.

Darlene and Butch built a house in another location nearby, and Tammy, their daughter, and her family, now live in the double-wide trailer. Tammy told her husband about the strange happenings at the old house and their trailer. Her husband went to the closet and told the spirit to show itself to him. At that very moment, a cold rush of wind swept past him, and as Tammy and her children sat in the living room, the fire in the fireplace immediately went out.

Music From Heaven

In 2003, Darlene's husband's aunt, Helen Howard, passed away. Besides being family, Helen's daughter, Polly, and Darlene have been close friends for years. When Helen died, Zachary, Darlene's son, wrote Helen a letter. Darlene found the letter so touching that she decided to read it aloud at Helen's funeral.

During the funeral, Darlene got up and read the beautiful things Zachary had said to Helen. In Zachary's letter, he told Helen what a fine Christian she was and how glad he was that she could see her family and friends again. He wrote about how nice it must be to be reunited with her beloved husband, Jim. Helen had attended church her whole life and for many years, played the piano for her church.

After the funeral, Darlene returned home. She was emotionally drained and decided to take a nap. Darlene hadn't been asleep long when she awoke to the most beautiful music she ever heard. She heard instruments that she had never heard before. Above the other unknown instruments was the sound of a piano. Darlene got up to find the source of the music. She went through the house and found no television, radio, or stereo on. The music stopped and she went to finish her nap. As soon as she lay back down, the music started again.

That evening at supper, Darlene told her husband what she had heard. He rolled his eyes in disbelief, so she quit talking about it. As they were eating, Darlene could see the shadow of wings fluttering in the living room. She never mentioned this to her husband as he wouldn't have believed it anyway. Darlene called Polly and told her what she had seen and heard. Polly was pleased by Darlene's story and said that her mother was up in Heaven playing piano with the saints.

A couple of years later, Polly herself had the same experience. One day while lying down, beautiful music came from nowhere. This convinced Polly that her mother was playing the piano in Heaven.

This is not a ghost story. This is a story about an incredible experience Darlene Steele had at a time of religious awakening in her life. It was this story that made me decide to add all phenomenal experiences and not just the frightening ones in this book. A lot of encounters with the unexplained are religious in nature and rather than scary, can be incredibly inspirational, comforting, and life changing, as was this event.

The Vision

Darlene had gone to church and firmly believed in God since she was a small child, but did not get saved until she was 22 years old. She asked the Lord into her heart in the summer of 1976. She, her husband, and two children lived at Verda, Kentucky. She had been under strong conviction and had told several of her neighbors. With her consent, her neighbors sent a preacher and a friend to her home one day. The preacher was holding a revival at a nearby church called Yocum Creek Baptist Church. She welcomed the men into her home that day. She said the sinner's prayer and was forgiven of her sins. She had never felt so wonderful in her life and the entire room seemed to fill with radiant sunlight.

Soon after Darlene got saved, she began to see a vision. She could see normally, but in her mind, she could see an image of a man on a pedestal that she was certain was Jesus. He was glowing and a bright light shone from His face so brilliantly that she could not see His features. On either side of Jesus were two male figures that Darlene believes are her angels. They wore white robes, as did Jesus. Both of them appeared to have wings and had wavy hair. The angel on the left was bent down on one knee and the one on the right stood and held a large thick book. This vision stayed in her mind for 24 hours.

The next evening, Darlene, her mother-in-law, and her two children attended the revival at Yocum Creek Baptist Church. It was a warm sunny evening with only a few clouds in the sky.

During the revival, her neighbors got up and began to sing a hymn called "The Master of the Sea."

During this song, Darlene began to get a warm feeling she had never felt before. She began to hear the sound of thunder. She looked out the window and saw the same blue peaceful sky that had been there on her drive to the church. Darlene looked around and she could tell by the other people around her that she was the only one who could hear the sound of a storm. She found this very puzzling.

Suddenly, Darlene felt like getting up and shouting. Regretfully, she held onto her seat and did not move. It took all her strength to sit there. It was then that she was given another vision. This time, she could see nothing but the vision. She could see a small ship being tossed around on the ocean with huge waves pouring water onto its deck. There was a violent storm above the ship with black storm clouds and streaks of lightning shooting through them. She could see every detail of the ship, including the back of a man that she instantly knew was Jesus. He had long brown hair and wore a white robe with a scarlet sash. He never turned around so that she could see His face, but she knew Who He was.

His disciples were sitting in front of Him in a semi-circle and she could see the two men on each end very well. The man on the left side of Jesus had brown eyes, black curly hair, and a very short beard and mustache. The man on the right of Jesus had a long narrow face, brown eyes, and brown hair that was rather long and parted in the middle. None of the disciples ever took their eyes away from Jesus' face.

Jesus lifted His left arm high in the air and began to slowly move it to the right. As He did this, He began to erase the storm. Wherever His hand touched, it turned the sky from black and ominous to beautiful and blue. The ship was no longer tossing to and fro, but was floating peacefully in calm water. With one sweep of His hand, the sun was shining and the sky was clear. As soon as the sky was blue, the vision was gone and Darlene could now once again see the inside of the church. This was the first and last time Darlene ever had a vision of this magnitude, but she would love to experience something similar again.

The following stories are from Darlene's childhood and most took place in Michigan. This story is about Darlene's first experience with the paranormal.

The Boat

This happened in 1958 when Darlene was only four years old. At the time, she and her family lived on Allen Street in Dowagiac, Michigan. She lived across the street from her grandmother, that she and everyone else, called "Aunt Nina," which was pronounced "Aunt Nine." Aunt Nina had an old clock that had a picture of the ocean and three fishermen in a boat.

One day, Darlene sat in her kitchen floor playing with toys while her mother was mopping in a bedroom. Darlene began to hear men having a conversation. She looked around and there, on her kitchen wall, were the three fishermen in the boat. They were talking as they rowed the small boat and were traveling across the top of the kitchen wall. She watched as the small boat went out of sight and into another room. She told her mother what she saw, but because Darlene was so young, she passed it off as an overactive imagination. Darlene has never forgotten about the strange sight she saw so many years ago but still does not know what it means or how to explain it.

Mother's Voice

While growing up in Dowagiac, Michigan, Darlene lived by a huge field where she and her siblings loved to play. One summer day, Darlene, her siblings, and mother all decided to lie down for an afternoon nap. Soon, everyone was asleep except Darlene who was wide awake. After a while of trying to go to sleep, she realized it was useless and got up to go play.

Darlene went outside into the bright sunshine and headed toward the big field. She did not ask permission to go out and play, but she felt her mother would not mind. She walked about picking flowers and berries and having a wonderful time.

Darlene soon ventured far away from her house to an old oak tree. She was finding all sorts of things to do when she heard her mother's voice calling her name. She was farther away from her house than she should have been, so she quickly began running through the field toward home.

As she ran, Darlene could still hear her mother calling her name. She could see her house, but could not see her mother anywhere. She ran into the yard and looked all around for her mother. When she couldn't find her, she went inside the house to look and to her surprise, there was her mother and all her siblings still sound asleep.

After her mother awoke, Darlene asked her if she had gotten up and called for her. Her mother said she had not. Darlene feels that she was called out of that field for a reason, but what that reason may be, she will never know.

The Money Car

Darlene's family was never dirt poor. They always had a clean home and clothes. Occasionally, they did struggle to make ends meet and amazingly, at one time, the family car seemed to want to help her family.

In 1963, Darlene's father bought an older car that was white with red interior. One time when her family was having a hard time financially, Darlene felt drawn to the car. She went out and opened the door and in the back seat lay a bunch of coins. After collecting them all, it added up to over $3.00 and that really went a long ways in those days. Several weeks later, the family had no money to buy milk and bread, and sure enough, Darlene looked in the backseat and there was just enough money to buy the food they needed.

This went on for a couple of years, but only when the family was in desperate need. There was no explanation for it because the children were the only ones to ever ride in the backseat and they never had money of their own to lose. Other family members also found money in the seats and floorboards, but only if they really needed it.

The seller of the car had told Darlene's dad that the previous owner had died. Perhaps the wealthy owner wanted to reward the family for taking such good care of his car. Whatever the reason, the "money car" always provided much-needed cash to a needy family and to this day, they are still grateful and appreciate the help they received.

Darlene's paternal grandmother told her the story of Glenwood House. She has been in contact with relatives of the Norton family who claim it is true. Darlene has lived on Glenwood Road twice in her life, and both times, she and her family experienced strange occurrences. It is possible that the whole area is haunted. The Glenwood House still stands, but with the change of ownership, has been given a different name.

Glenwood House And Glenwood Road

There is a house in Dowagiac, Michigan formerly called the Glenwood House. In the early 1900s, the house was owned by a man named Billy Norton. Billy Norton lived alone with his dog.

According to Mr. Norton, one day, he was at his home when he saw a lady with long black hair and a flowing gown floating down his stairway. It frightened him so badly that he broke his front door getting out. He ran four miles into town without ever stopping. His dog stayed right with him the whole time.

Many people remembered and talked about the day that Billy Norton, with his dog right behind him, came running into town telling of an apparition coming down his stairs.

In 1966 when Darlene was 12 years old, she and her family moved into a house on Glenwood Road near the Glenwood House. The previous owners of the house only lived there about a year and did not finish it. The basement was the only part of the house that was livable. Darlene and her family moved into the basement while the rest of the house was being completed. Because they could not afford a carpenter, Darlene's parents worked on the house themselves. This was a very slow process and the family lived a long time in the basement. Darlene and her siblings didn't mind at all and in fact, they enjoyed living there.

Darlene remembers well the exact day that she moved into the basement of the house on Glenwood Road. It was July 2, 1966. This was also her 12th birthday. That day, Darlene was in the kitchen when a strange feeling came over her. As she was at the stove making Cream of Wheat, she was certain that she had done this same thing exactly some time before. She distinctly recalled cooking Cream of Wheat in that kitchen wearing the same clothes. She knew it was impossible because that was her first day in that house.

Shortly after moving in, Darlene's parents found bones in the room that was to be Darlene's bedroom. Apparently, the people who lived there before left them behind. The bones were bound together by strips of cloth and resembled wind chimes. Darlene wondered if the former residents were practicing voodoo there. No one in her family knew what kind of bones they were. Darlene's mother insisted that her father burn and bury them immediately.

Darlene and her sister, Cheryl, slept in a bed that was near the basement stairs that led up to the main level of the house. On the second day there, Darlene awoke at 8:00 am to hear the basement door above her creak open. She assumed it was one of her parents. She then heard someone take three steps down the stairs. She turned to see who it was, but there was no one there and the basement door was closed. She got up and discovered everyone asleep in their beds. This event seemed to be a preview of many strange experiences that Darlene and her family would have in this house.

Several months later, Darlene and her siblings came home to find their mother very pale and upset. Darlene asked her mother what was wrong, but she said nothing. Later, she asked her mother again why she seemed bothered. Her mother reluctantly told her that earlier, while she was in the kitchen washing dishes, she heard the basement door open. She froze in fear when she heard someone running down the stairs. While she stood there, a man in a military uniform, carrying a rifle, walked by her and went in a bedroom. He never acknowledged her presence. She could see the door that led outside and no one ever went out. Assuming the man was still in the bedroom, she cautiously walked to the doorway and looked in, but the room was empty.

One afternoon, Darlene was standing in front of a full-length mirror brushing her hair. Her mother was sitting on the bed behind her and they were talking. Darlene would occasionally glance at her mother through the mirror. Then, in the mirror, Darlene saw the dark silhouette of a man. He was walking behind her. He had mutton chops and a long split tail coat. Darlene quickly turned around. No one was in the room with her except her mother. Darlene turned back around and still, she could see the man's image in the mirror.

Darlene's youngest sister, Denise, claimed to have seen a blue-and-white checked shirt float across the basement. Although she was very young at the time, the others took note of it due to the other strange happenings.

After many months, the house was completed and everyone moved upstairs. Shortly after, Darlene's sister, Cheryl, got up in the middle of the night while everyone else slept soundly. Suddenly, everyone was awakened by a blood curdling scream. Everyone ran to the room where Cheryl was. She said that a man with a split tail coat, buckled shoes, and mutton chops came walking toward her. When she screamed, he disappeared. The man Cheryl described perfectly fit the description of the man Darlene had seen in the mirror two years before. Darlene had never told her sister about seeing the man in the mirror.

On another occasion, Darlene awoke in the middle of the night and saw a figure that looked like a skeleton hovering over Cheryl, who was asleep in her bed. The figure was directly above Cheryl and its head was right above hers. It was in the same position as she was. Darlene could not wait until the next morning to tell her sister. This, of course, frightened Cheryl who was only seven years old at the time.

In the fall of the 1967, Darlene's ten-year-old brother, Donald, had gotten up one Saturday morning and put on a pair of tan pants and matching tan shirt. Donald grew bored and wanted to go to his friend's house and play. Their mother told Donald to call his friend and make sure it was okay. He called his friend and a visit would be fine. Donald didn't want to worry about soiling his good clothes, so he changed into his play clothes, but kept on his new white tennis shoes. He hopped on his bike and headed to his friend's house which was about half a mile away on a farm.

About an hour later, Darlene and her two sisters went down to the basement. Since they lived down there for a while, it was now the perfect place to play. The windows of the basement were set up high on the walls and were just at ground level outside. The three sisters were sitting playing when they saw their brother walk past one of the windows. Since the windows were at ground level, they could only see him from the waist down. He had on his tan pants and white tennis shoes. The family dog, Zing, was trotting behind him wagging his tail. Zing was part collie and very protective of his family, as well as their home and property. He was a great watch-dog and never allowed a stranger into the yard. He barked viciously at anyone who came around and would have to be restrained when visitors approached.

At the same time, the three girls remembered that Donald had changed clothes and went to a friend's house. They ran upstairs to Donald's room and there lay his tan pants and matching shirt on the bed. They ran and told their mother and she said that Donald had not come home. Darlene called the home where Donald was visiting and asked to speak to him. She was told that he was playing in the barn and having a good time. The mother of Donald's friend told Darlene to call back and she would let the boys answer the phone in the barn. Darlene hung up the phone and dialed the number again. After a few rings, Donald answered the phone. Darlene considers this to be one of the strangest experiences she ever had.

Around that same time, Darlene's two younger sisters were playing in the backyard. Donald was again visiting friends. Her dad was at work, and she and her mother were inside. According to her sisters, their red ball came slowly floating over their two-story house and landed where they were playing. The girls quickly ran around to the front of the house and found no one there. Darlene's younger sisters also said that one day they went into the living room to find the rocking chair rocking by itself.

Cheryl found it quite a thrill to run down the hallway into Darlene's room, leap high in the air, and land on Darlene's bed. Because it was very dangerous and likely she'd eventually break the bed down, Cheryl was scolded every time she did this. Although she was not allowed to perform her daring "bed leaping" trick, Cheryl could not help but continue to do it. She was still doing it, just more quietly or when no one was inside. It is very hard to be silent when doing such a thing, so it was pretty evident when she was "sneaking" down the hall and jumping on the bed.

One day, it occurred to Darlene that she had not heard Cheryl leaping on the bed in a while. Since she loved to do it so much, Darlene found it curious that her sister had stopped. The scolding did not seem to make much of a difference, so she wondered why Cheryl had suddenly stopped on her own. Darlene asked Cheryl about it and her sister told her that one day, after she had ran down the hall and got her speed up, she burst into Darlene's room and leaped on the bed. While she was in mid-air, she noticed a man with a blue-and-white checked shirt sitting in the corner by Darlene's bed. Her face went in the mattress as she landed and when she looked up again, the man was gone. Cheryl told Darlene that the man frightened her so that she was afraid to run into her room anymore.

For years, Donald claimed to see a little boy with blonde hair and green eyes in the basement. He never saw the boy when the family was living down there. It was only after they moved upstairs that he began seeing him. The boy looked between ten and twelve years old. Donald chased the little boy when he saw him, but quickly the little boy would vanish. Donald would always go upstairs and tell Darlene when he saw the boy. Darlene could tell by his eyes and expression that he was telling the truth.

After three years of living in the house at Glenwood Road, all of the strange experiences suddenly stopped. No one knows why, but nothing unusual ever happened there again.

Years later, in 1984, Darlene and her family moved from Evarts, Kentucky, to her hometown of Dowagiac, Michigan. Darlene, her husband, and children moved to Glenwood, right off Glenwood Road, which was very close to the house she once lived in as a child. After two years of living in Michigan, they decided to move back to Evarts. Darlene's husband, Butch, went back to Kentucky first to get his construction business running again. Darlene and the kids would move back later when things were better organized.

During this time apart, Darlene and her children decided to go to Evarts and visit Butch for a day or two. Darlene's mother, who had been staying with them after Butch's departure, stayed and took care of their house at Glenwood.

After Darlene arrived at Evarts, she called her mother to check on things. Darlene's mother was rather distressed sounding. She told Darlene that she had slept in the children's bunk bed and it began shaking and making noises in the middle of the night. Darlene told her mother that it may be unsafe and to not sleep in it any more. Her mother had sounded very upset, so Darlene decided to cut her visit short and go back to Michigan to check on her.

Upon arrival back to her house, Darlene went immediately and looked at the bunk bed. It seemed sturdy and in good condition. That night around 3:00 am, Darlene was awakened by a dreadful sound. She sprang to her feet and went running toward it. It was coming from the bedroom where the bunk bed was.

She went in to find the bed shaking violently. From the bed came the sounds of a train, glass breaking, and a loud buzzing all at once. After about a minute, the shaking and sounds stopped.

There was not a train track anywhere close and the sounds were coming directly from the bed. There was an Amtrak train track about an eighth of a mile away, but Darlene had never heard the trains on it. The Amtrak was a modern, smooth, quiet running train. The sound of this one was like the old rattling steam engines that created a chugging sound. Needless to say, the bunk bed did not go back to Kentucky when the family moved.

In 1997, Darlene's mother moved to Harlan County and lived in an apartment on Ivy Hill. Once, while Darlene was visiting, her mother told her that she had seen a man in a blue-and-white checked shirt walk toward her from the kitchen and then disappear. Darlene could not help but remember both of her sister's experiences with a blue-and-white checked shirt at Glenwood Road.

Many inexplicable things happened to Darlene and her family while living in the houses on Glenwood Road. Recently, Darlene's mother told her that, on one occasion, she saw the silhouette of a man on the ceiling above her bed. These are not all of the occurrences there. Darlene's mother says that she had many experiences there that she would rather not talk about.

Darlene does not believe in reincarnation. She believes that God gives you one life to live and then you must face judgment. She believes your soul goes to Heaven and upon death, you do not live subsequent lives. I have an explanation for this story. I believe that all our ancestors' life experiences are in their DNA and passed on to us and at times, we can feel what they felt and remember what they experienced.

Memories Of "The Big City"

As a very young child, Darlene seemed to have memories of another life. She told she and her family lived in a big city that she called "New York City." She gave detailed descriptions of them going to market and in one instance, going to court. She described her home in this big city with a vividness that was a bit disturbing to her mother who knew her daughter had never lived in such a place. As Darlene grew older, many memories of living in the big city began to fade.

As soon as Darlene's younger brother, Donald, began to talk, he began to tell about when he lived in what he called "The Big City." He began to describe the same things Darlene had earlier. As Donald grew older, he, too, forgot about "The Big City." Now, all they seem to have are memories of discussing it as children. It would be interesting to see if any of their family before them really lived in such a place.

In June 1964, a monster began terrorizing the area of Dowagiac, Michigan, and did so the entire summer. People began finding large footprints around their homes and many claim to have had encounters with this monster that was most commonly called the "Sister Lakes Monster" because of the region where it was said to roam. It has also been called the "Dewey Lake Monster," "Silver Creek Monster," and "Magician Lake Monster." The first sightings were by migrant workers, but soon, there were so many reports of sightings that it was hard for the police to investigate them all.

Police began patrolling night and day to make residents feel safer. All who claimed to have seen this monster said that it was big and black, with red, glowing eyes. One family said that their dog approached the monster and was blinded by the bright red eyes. The monster made national news and soon, the "Sister Lakes Monster" hysteria began with local businesses using the monster for advertisement and restaurants serving "monster burgers."

Although many enjoyed the new found fame of the Dowagiac, Michigan, area and exploited it to make money, many lived for months in terror, especially the children. After that summer, the sightings ceased and everything calmed down. Now, all that is left of the monster is the plaster molds made of the footprints and the memories of those who experienced the wild summer of 1964.

Sister Lakes Monster

Darlene Steele was nine years old when the sightings of a monster began. She and her brother, Donald, were outside playing one warm June morning in the area behind their house that all the local children called "the back alley." It wasn't really an alley, just a dirt road behind the house. As the children played, they noticed strange tracks in the dirt road. They were very long and wide. The children were trying to identify the tracks when their Uncle Chuck drove up and pulled in their driveway. Uncle Chuck didn't visit very often, so Darlene and Donald feared something bad had happened. Their mother must have thought the same thing because she quickly met her brother-in-law in the yard. The first thing Uncle Chuck said was, "Get the kids inside and keep them in the house." All three found this very odd.

Uncle Chuck went on to say that there were credible people claiming they had seen a nine-foot, hairy creature roaming the area. This terrified Darlene and Donald, and they quickly remembered the footprints in the back alley. Their mother found the whole thing preposterous. She did not heed Uncle Chuck's warning and simply went back in to continue whatever she was doing. She did not make Darlene and Donald come inside, but they did anyway. There was no way they were staying outside with a nine-foot monster!

The two children stayed inside all day and could not wait for their father to come home from work, so they could tell him about the monster. Finally, their dad arrived and they ran to him and told him what his brother, Chuck, had said. Their father laughed and said that he had already heard about the monster and didn't believe a single word of it and they shouldn't either. He told his children not to worry about a silly monster and to go out and play and have fun. Darlene and Donald did not. They stayed inside most of that summer. Uncle Chuck believed it and they did, too.

They lived on the road that led to Dewey Lake where a lot of the sightings occurred. They also lived near the swamp where it was said to be hiding out. There was no way Darlene and Donald would take a chance of being captured by this horrible beast. After awhile, the two children began to venture outside into the yard a little. They kept a good distance from bushes or anywhere that would make a good hiding place for the monster.

Reports of the monster were flooding in from the entire Sister Lakes region. The Sister Lakes Monster was all the rage. Everyone was talking about it and film crews were set up everywhere desperately trying to get footage of the creature.

Aunt Nina, Darlene's grandmother, firmly believed in the monster and her belief fueled Darlene's terror.

One day at the grocery store, Darlene and Donald noticed a sketch of the monster hanging outside on the storefront. It was a sketch to warn people about the monster. Darlene thought it was the scariest picture she had ever seen. Her mother came out of the store telling of a man who was inside describing his personal encounter with the monster.

By July, "monster mania" had taken hold of Dowagiac, Michigan. Walter Cronkite was on the CBS Evening News talking about the creature. Hunters with high-powered rifles were pouring in from everywhere to try to kill the monster. Soon, the hunters were more of a threat to people than the monster itself. There was a 6:00 pm curfew placed on residents of Dowagiac and Darlene was convinced it was because of the monster. She later learned it was because of the over-zealous hunters that were shooting at anything that moved.

Someone claimed to have seen the monster come out of Swisher Woods and onto Swisher Street to eat berries. It wasn't long before an ABC film crew had set up cameras on Swisher Street to try to catch the monster on film. Others soon joined the film crew to try to catch a glimpse of the beast. Needless to say, the Sister Lakes Monster never made an appearance on Swisher Street again.

All the grownups that believed in the monster confirmed its existence with Darlene and she could not understand her parents' disbelief in it. One day, a girl that Darlene went to school with claimed that she was walking with two of her friends in the woods near her home when the monster ran across the path in front of her. This was only a fourth of a mile from Darlene's home. The girls' photo was on the front page of the local newspaper and Darlene cut it out and kept it as a reminder that she, too, could have an encounter with the monster if she didn't stay inside her yard.

Darlene's house didn't have air conditioning and her family slept with the windows open and fans on. Darlene slept by an open window and her sister, Denise, slept with her. One night in late July, Darlene was awakened by a car. She looked out the window by her bed and saw that it was a police car in the back alley. The police car pulled out onto the main road and circled the neighborhood. It was going rather fast and Darlene was sure it was chasing the monster. The police car circled the neighborhood several times and then left. Darlene wished it wouldn't leave because she felt safer with it there. The monster must be hiding in her neighborhood. She was too scared to go back to sleep, so she just lay there without moving.

Suddenly, she heard something scratching on the screen of her window and then, the sound of the screen ripping. She quickly sat up and saw something with glowing eyes peering back at her. Terrified, Darlene jumped over her sister and ran to her parents' bedroom. She tried to wake them up, but they were sleeping too soundly. Darlene thought about her little sister in her bedroom and visualized a big hairy arm reaching through the window and scooping her up. She mustered up the courage to go back into her bedroom. Upon entering, she realized that nothing was outside the window and her sister was safe in bed. Darlene thought the monster must have left and lay back down by her sister. She lay awake until daylight listening for the monster to return. Luckily, it did not.

Sometime that morning, Darlene fell asleep. When she awoke, she told her mother what had happened the night before. Her mother listened, but Darlene could tell that she doubted the whole thing. Darlene insisted that she and her mother go out and inspect the back of the house. There, on the side of the house, were four large claw marks. The screen that was intact the day before was now partially torn and hanging off of the window. A huge branch, from high in a tree, had been snapped off and laid in the yard. Darlene's mother could not deny what she had seen and from that time on, began to wonder of the validity of the Sister Lakes Monster.

At the end of summer, two young men claimed to see the monster heading north and from that point on, there were no more sightings. By the time school started back that fall, things had gotten back to normal and monster mania had settled down considerably. The girl that encountered the monster got to tell about it in class. She told of a huge beast running out in front of her and her friends, ripping a huge limb from a tree, and throwing it wildly. She described how terrified she was and how one of her friends fainted right there in the woods. She told her story so truthfully that even doubters had a hard time not believing in the monster.

Darlene survived that strange summer in 1964 without being attacked by the vicious creature. Although it must have been stressful for a child to endure, she can now say that she encountered the infamous Sister Lakes Monster.

Getting into the Monster Act

THE PEOPLE and authorities of the Sister Lakes region in Southwestern Michigan breathed easier Monday, with the crowds of curious and tourists gone and only the "Monster of Sister Lakes" to worry about. But while the weekend crowds were in the area the merchants and roadside establishments were not loath to cash in a bit on the publicity that has followed the first report on the "nine-foot, 500-pound" monster of a week ago. Reid's drive-in restaurant at Sister Lakes enticed tourists with a stuffed monster and offerings of "monster brew" and "monster burgers," above and at right below. A monster trap put in its appearance in front of the home of Dawn Grabemeyer, of rural Dowagiac near Dewey Lake, lower left.

The next are stories from Darlene's family. None of these events happened to her personally. Some of the stories happened over a hundred years ago, while others happened recently. All were told by honest people and all are true.

The Icy Hand

Darlene's mother was originally from Hartselle, Alabama. She had been married briefly and had a child before she met Darlene's father. Her mother was first married when she was twenty years old, and after a short and miserable marriage, she and her small child came back home to live with her parents.

Her parents' house was two stories and her parents' bedroom had always been upstairs. After many years of bad health, her mother could no longer climb the stairs to her bedroom, so she slept downstairs while her husband still slept upstairs. Darlene's mother also slept downstairs and her baby daughter slept with her.

One night, Darlene's mother was lying in bed. Suddenly, an icy cold hand grabbed hers. The bedroom was completely dark and she could see nothing. She did not move or make a sound. The hand continued to hold onto her. She strained her eyes to see in the dark, but could not. She continued to lie completely still. She was terrified and the hand was absolutely freezing. The icy hand held hers for a long time. Finally, it let go. She sprung to the floor and ran to get her mother in the next room.

She and her mother turned on every light in the house and searched everywhere for an intruder. All the doors and windows were still locked, just as they had been before they went to bed. They never figured out what was in the house that night or how it got in, but thankfully, it never happened again.

Darlene's paternal grandmother told her this story. This was a family story that was passed down through the years.

The Phantom Ball

Some of Darlene's ancestors made their way from Alabama to Michigan as early as the late 1800s. After their relocation to Michigan, it was necessary to make another trip back to Alabama for more of their belongings. Moving was extremely difficult without the convenience of cars. Everything had to be packed on horses and carriages.

Three men were chosen to make the long trip back to Alabama. It would take them many days to get there and they would have to find shelter at night along the way. Back in those days, it was common practice to find a home and ask the residents if you could spend the night with them or sleep in their barn. You would be welcomed into the home and probably invited to have dinner with the family.

After a couple days' travel, the men were now in Rolling Prairie, Indiana. It was getting late in the day, so they began looking for a place to spend the night. They were in a very secluded area of the state and houses were separated by many miles. At sundown, they spied a large home off in the distance. They knew this would probably be the last house before nightfall, so they began crossing large fields and meadows to get to it.

Upon arrival, the men realized the house was vacant. It appeared no one had lived there for quite some time. The men decided that would be as good a place as any to spend the night. They were tired and the house would keep them dry and safe.

The men discovered that the front door was open. It was a grand home with high ceilings and large rooms. They wondered why such a fine home was not occupied. They built a fire in one of the large fireplaces, sat by it, and ate from their knapsacks.

After spreading their wool blankets on the wooden floor, the men were soon sound asleep.

It is hard to say what time it was, but the fire had long been out. The men were awakened by the sound of music. Startled, they sat up quickly and looked around. To their amazement, the big room was aglow with candlelight. Loud music could be heard throughout the house. The room that was bare and scantily furnished was now lavishly decorated with French furniture and Austrian crystal. There, in the room with them, was a man and woman dressed in fashions that were in style in the late 1700s. The couple danced joyously around the room and gazed directly into each other's eyes. They were smiling as they danced and acted as if they were the only ones in the room.

The three men didn't even bother to go out the front door. They jumped out the nearest window, ran to their horses, and got far away from the house as quickly as possible.

The men finally made it to Alabama and after getting what they came for, started on the long journey back to Michigan. They took a longer, rougher route back home so they would not have to pass by the vacant house that gave them such a scare on their trip south.

The Angel

Darlene's father, Jake Milton Clardy, lived in Arkansas in the 1940s. He was married before he married Darlene's mother. His first wife had two children, a girl and boy, from a previous relationship. Soon, they had three more children together. The three children they had together were girls.

Jake's wife became sick. They soon learned that she was terminally ill and did not have long to live. In her last days, his wife spent most of the time asleep in bed. It was obvious that she was on her death bed and the end was near. During this time, the dipper that they used to dip drinking water began to beat against the pail that was used to carry water from the well. The dipper would rattle against the pail quite often.

When his wife was in her last hours of life, Jake and his stepson sat on the front porch. The daughters were taking turns sitting with their dying mother. As Jake and his stepson sat there, a beautiful woman walked out of the garden and approached the porch. She began to slowly rise into the air. Jake called for his daughters to hurry outside. Darlene's oldest half sister said that when she got outside, she could see something rising high in the air. Their father told them to always remember that a beautiful angel came and got their mother and took her to Heaven. When they went back inside, their mother had died.

Big Joe

Darlene had a great uncle that everyone called "Big Joe." He was strong, active, and always wore an English driving hat. Big Joe was actually her stepfather's uncle and the person he was named after.

Big Joe died when Darlene was 13 years old. Although she never saw it with her own eyes, other family members claimed that Big Joe could make a table rise and dance around in the air.

In the mid-1920s, Uncle Joe and his family traveled to northern Michigan to visit relatives. They were there for several days and spent nights at the relatives' home. While he was there, Big Joe had turned in for the night and was lying down in a bed. After a few minutes, an unseen powerful hand grabbed his neck and pinned him down to the bed. It held him down for several minutes before letting go.

Big Joe, as well as other family members, often spoke of this terrifying event.

According to Darlene's family, this happened in the late 1800s in Decatur, Alabama. This story was passed down through the years by her relatives on the Sandlin side of her family.

Mother's Ghost

A farmer went to plant corn in his cornfield one day and headed out with his plow and horses. His mother, who had been ill for a long time, was sitting on the porch in her favorite rocking chair as she did most every day.

After several hours of plowing, the farmer's horses began to act odd and rear up. At that moment, he saw his mother standing in front of the horses. She was wearing a black dress with a black veil over her face. He wondered how his mother, in such poor health, could have walked all the way out in the field. He was curious why she was dressed so unlike she normally dressed. He began to walk toward her and she disappeared.

The man ran home because he knew something strange was going on. He breathed a sigh of relief when he saw his mother still sitting in her rocking chair, but his relief was short-lived. As he approached her, he realized that she had passed away while sitting in her chair.

The Dancing Figures

Darlene's Aunt Betty was her mother's youngest sister. Her mother's family was from Austinville, Alabama, which was eventually annexed with Decatur, Alabama. Darlene's mother, Martha, is nearly five years older than Betty. Martha has black hair, brown eyes, and an olive complexion, while Betty has red hair, green eyes, and fair skin.

Martha and Betty's parents were Ola Clyde Sandlin and Lona Amanda Moss Sandlin. Grandpa Sandlin was a farmer and he leased many acres of land to grow cotton, corn, and other cash crops. He also worked as a mechanic. He was tall, dark, and had a square jaw. Grandma Sandlin was a hard working mother and housewife. She cooked three square meals a day. She got the family's milk from a cow named Daisy, raised a garden for food, canned vegetables for winter, cleaned feverishly, sewed all the family's clothing, churned butter, and cooked everything from scratch. Grandma Sandlin had long black hair with streaks of gray, and brown eyes.

The Sandlins were the first in their community to own modern appliances and a television set. Grandma got upset with Grandpa when he surprised her with a modern cooking stove. She was afraid he had spent too much money. The Sandlins loved to go to socials where there was food, music, dancing, and other fun activities.

Once a year, Darlene and her family would travel to Alabama and visit her grandparents. Grandpa and Uncle Garland would catch catfish from the river and have a big fish fry. There would be homemade hush puppies and a huge feast topped off with homemade ice cream. By that time, they had moved to a farm in Hartselle, Alabama.

This happened in 1939 while the family was still in Austinville. Martha was nine years old and Betty was five. Martha and Betty went outside in December without anyone knowing it. They played in the freezing weather without coats. As a result, Martha got pleurisy and Betty had double pneumonia. At that time, pleurisy was serious, but pneumonia was deadly. Because there were no antibiotics, there was nothing to fight the infection.

In those days in the country, people were treated in their homes and doctors would come to their patients' houses. Dr. Erskine Chenault was the local doctor. He was a loved and respected individual in the community. He informed the Sandlins that little Betty may not survive her illness. Dr. Chenault placed Betty on the living room sofa and created a homemade oxygen tent out of a brand of material called Sullivan. Sullivan was similar to today's plastic.

Betty's condition became critical. Her temperature kept getting higher and she was near death. Members of the Sandlin's church, the Church of Christ, all came and prayed for Betty.

When Betty was at her worst, Grandma Sandlin looked out her window and saw three short dark figures dancing underneath the clothesline. She could not believe her eyes. She did not have time to go outside and look because her child was so ill. She kept inviting local people in her home to pray for her daughter. All the while, she continued to look out and see these dancing figures. Concerned about the figures, Grandma Sandlin kept looking out the window. To her surprise, the figures were now on the porch dancing just like they had under the clothesline.

Another time, she looked out and they were right under the window. They were completely dark, like shadow people. They were small and seemed to pay no mind to the activities in the house. They continued to dance all through the night.

The Sandlins stayed up all night with Betty. Her fever would not go down. They prayed for her recovery and the dancing figures stayed outside all night long.

Near daybreak, Betty's fever broke and she made a quick turn for the better. To her family's relief, she opened her eyes and spoke. Delighted in her daughter's improved condition, Grandma Sandlin went to see what the figures were that had danced all night long, but they had gone.

During the days of Betty's illness, Dr. Chenault visited her 22 times. She made a full recovery. She still remembers being in the oxygen tent and seeing the members of her church praying for her through the thick clear material.

Both Grandma and Grandpa Sandlin were of Native American descent, and one can only speculate if the dancing figures were relatives of long ago, in ceremony, asking the Creator for Betty's recovery.

Darlene's father, Joe, had two brothers, Chuck and Todd. She has heard all three of them tell this story while she was growing up.

Indian Lake Ghost

Joe, Chuck, and Todd had heard for years, that at a certain place at Indian Lake in Dowagiac, Michigan, between the hours of midnight and 2:00 am, you could see a man walk out of the water, continue up on shore, and then disappear. Supposedly, the man had drowned in Indian Lake years before. The three brothers decided to test the story to see if it was true.

They chose a clear and moonlit night. They arrived early at 10:00 pm and parked their car facing the exact place on the lake in which the apparition was supposed to emerge. The three sat waiting and watching. They watched for hours with no luck. Growing tired and bored, they had decided to call it a night when they spotted something moving in the water. All three watched with their hearts beating violently as a figure walked from the water and onto the shore. It stood there for a few seconds, and then disappeared. Chuck started the car and sped out as quickly as he could. The three brothers never dared to return to that spot of the lake again.

On another occasion, the three brothers were riding in their car in the Dowagiac, Michigan area when they came across two men hitchhiking. Chuck decided to offer the two a ride and pulled over on the side of the road. There was no sign of the two men, and it was such an open area that they couldn't have run anywhere and hid. The three brothers got out of the car and searched for the two men, but there wasn't anyone anywhere.

Darlene's dad and uncles told about this for years. They puzzled over where the two men could have gone so suddenly and how they seemed to disappear in a matter of seconds.

Clara

Darlene's father, Joe, had a sister named Clara. In the 1920s, when Clara was only twelve years old, she was sent to the store to get something for her mother. It was a warm summer day, so Clara went barefoot. On her way there, she came upon a rusty tin can. She kicked it out of the road and when she did, she cut her toe. This tiny cut led to a then-deadly disease, tetanus. The child became ill and eventually died.

Forty years later, in the 1960s, Joe began to experience heart problems. One day while at his mother's house, he had a heart attack. Joe claimed that while he was having the heart attack, Clara appeared to him and was beckoning him to go with her. He said that she was still a child and wearing the same gray dress she had been buried in many years ago.

Darlene's two sisters and daughter have seen what they call "the Indian." Darlene has never seen this spirit before.

The Indian

In 1981, Darlene's daughter, Tammy, was outside in the yard playing with her grandfather and cousins. Tammy came in very excited and told her mother that she had just seen an "Indian."

Darlene asked her ten-year-old daughter to describe what she saw. Tammy said that she saw a Native American man running on the knob behind their house. He had some sort of weapon or tool in his hand and looked like he might be hunting. She said she only saw his profile.

Not long after that, Tammy told Darlene that she saw the same Indian man standing in her bedroom behind the door. This time, she got a better look at him and described him as being older, with dark skin, and graying black hair that was not in braids, but rolled very unusually.

In 1982, Darlene awoke one night to find Tammy in the corner of her bedroom. Tammy told her that she was scared and Darlene told her to come and get in bed with her. The next morning, Tammy told Darlene that she woke up in the middle of the night not feeling well. When she awoke, she discovered an Indian woman sitting in the floor of her room. The woman had long black hair and was leaning against the wall near Tammy's bed. The woman's arms were reaching toward the ceiling and she was gazing up at it. While the Indian woman sat in her floor, another person wearing an orange wool coat walked into her room and went in her closet. She could hear clothes hangers hitting each other as this person moved around.

Tammy ran out and left both of them in her room. She ran into her parents' bedroom and that is where Darlene found her. Tammy also said that while she was in bed with Darlene and Butch, she saw the old shriveled up hand of an elderly woman lying on the bed with them.

Several years later, Darlene learned that while her youngest sister, Denise, was visiting her in 1978, she encountered what sounded like the same spirit of the Indian man. He was standing in the bedroom in which Denise was staying, and she was so frightened that she threw a blanket over her head. When she pushed the blanket back down, he was gone.

Denise was not the first to see this spirit. In 1977, Darlene's other sister, Cheryl, was at her grandmother's house in Michigan when she looked out a window and saw the Indian man dancing under a streetlight. Later, she looked out of the same window and saw the Indian man looking back at her.

In the late 1980s, Tammy was visiting a friend in Michigan when she awoke to find a man with long black hair raking his fingernails over her stomach. He was similar in appearance to the man she saw behind her door in Kentucky. Her friend, who was in the room with her, awoke to see the man sitting on the bed and holding his hands at Tammy's stomach. After telling her parents what she'd seen, the friend's parents checked all doors and windows and they were all locked.

Many years later, after Tammy is grown and married, she and her husband have moved to Texas. One day at her home, Tammy saw the Indian man once again standing behind a door.

No one knows why the spirit of this Native American man keeps appearing to certain family members or what his significance may be. It will be interesting to see where he shows up next.

Everyone calls Darlene's husband "Butch." This happened to Butch in 1960, when he was 12 years old. He claims to not believe in ghosts.

Papaw Steele

Butch Steele grew up at Red Bud Hill in Evarts. He still lives there today. One summer night, he and two of his friends were sitting on a porch in the Black Mountain community looking up at the starry sky. He and his friends noticed something on a bridge that is located on Highway 215 and is close to the new Black Mountain School. They could see something glowing on this bridge. The three of them sat and watched the glowing object. The glowing object began to take shape and soon, it took the form of a man with a top hat and cane. The boys jumped up and quickly ran into the house. Butch never saw anything like that again.

Butch's father, Pleas Elijah Steele, also claimed to not believe in ghosts. One night in the late 1970s, he got up and saw a white "thing" that darted out of a back room and went through the front door. He said this white object was small and got bigger in back. It was floating well off of the ground as it shot through his house. He spoke of this for many years.

Zachary Steele was very close to his grandfather, Pleas Elijah. "Papaw Steele" always told Zachary that one day he would live in and own the old Steele home. Zachary firmly believed this. He never doubted for a second that this would not happen because it was his beloved grandfather's solemn promise. Several years after the passing of Papaw Steele, a chain of events lead to just that, and now, Zachary and his family own and live on the old Steele property.

In May 1994, Zachary claimed to see a perfectly round black ball sail through the front yard of his home on Red Bud Hill. Zachary's sister, Tammy, also claimed to have an unusual experience around that same time. She claimed to awake in the middle of the night to feel a hand caress the side of her cheek.

Pleas Elijah's daughter, Luada, said that she, too, had an experience at that same time. She awoke one night to see a very young version of her father standing in the bedroom doorway. He looked just the way he did when Luada was a child. He was very handsome and his hair was shiny black. He was smiling and his teeth were dazzling white. On May 28, 1994, Papaw Steele passed away.

In 2003, as Butch was cutting wood, he began to cut a piece from a dangerous position. Suddenly, he felt a hand touch his right shoulder even though no one else was there. This made Butch decide to stop and cut the wood in a safer manner. On another occasion, Butch's sister, Luada, was cutting grass at the old Steele home place. Although no one was living there, she couldn't stand to see her parents' home to look unkempt. As she was mowing, she felt a hand touch her right shoulder. She looked around and no one was there. She was at a spot that Papaw Steele was leery of. Both Luada and Butch feel that their father's spirit is still looking out for them and protecting them.

The old bridge at Black Mountain has now been replaced.

Darlene says her father told this story many times and claimed to have seen it himself.

The Model-T Ford

In the early 1900s, a family in Michigan was doing very well financially. Their small business was prospering and they were considered to be one of the wealthier families of the area. A man and his son ran the business and both were making a good living for their families. With all the advantages that wealth brings, it also brings negative aspects as well. People who are considered to have money can become a target of criminals, as was the case of this family.

The father and son business partners were coming home from work one night. They lived in a large home and drove a new vehicle that was very modern for the day. Having a "horseless carriage" was considered a luxury.

The rest of the family was gone on a long vacation, so the men were coming home to an empty house, or so they thought. It seems that some local criminals decided to take advantage of the men being alone. They broke into the house and waited for them to come home, assuming that the men would have the earnings of that day with them.

Unsuspecting, the father and son drove their Model-T Ford down their driveway and got out as they did every evening. They entered their home, and no one really knows exactly how it came about, but both men were found dead in the home the next day. They had been the victims of a robbery. It is unknown if they were killed immediately or held hostage for a period of time. The robbers were never caught.

After that gruesome event, the family quickly moved out of the house that now carried such bad memories. It was put up for sale at a low price, and even though it was one of the finest homes around, no one wanted to move in it. For years, the house sat empty.

Even though no one lived in the house, Darlene's father, as well as other people in the community, claimed to see the lights and hear the engine of the Model-T Ford coming down the driveway. The lights would go out and the sound of the motor would stop at the site of an old well. This happened frequently for many years after the double murder took place.

The Crimson Robe

In 1985, Butch Steele got a job in Kingsport, Tennessee, doing construction work. He still lived in Harlan County, so he commuted every day. Sometimes, he started work very early and left late. In the winter of 1985, Butch was on his way home to Harlan County. He was on Highway 19 and had just taken the Big Stone Gap, Virginia exit, when he dozed off at the wheel of his 1975 Ford Pinto.

When he dozed off, Butch clearly saw a man wearing a crimson robe standing before him. As soon as he saw this man, he immediately woke up. Butch awoke to find he was going 60 miles per hour toward a stop sign. Luckily, he was able to stop just in time. If he had not, Butch would have driven straight into the side of a cliff and possibly been killed. Butch contributes this as divine protection from Heaven and believes that the man in the crimson robe was Jesus Himself.

The Sparrow

Darlene's mother-in-law, Sally Steele, lost her mother when she was very young. Sally's mother was only 38 years old when she died. Years before, she told Sally that, after her death, if she was ever needed, she would come back in the form of a bird.

Right before the death of her mother, when Sally was nine years old, Sally dreamed that she was riding in a hearse. The hearse approached a railroad track and began to rock back and forth. Sally told her mother about the dream and her mother told her it was a sign of death. Sure enough, a few days later, Sally's mother died.

Years passed and Sally and her family went through very hard times. Her husband, Pleas Elijah Steele, was injured in the war and went a long time without working. He continued to have illnesses and could not keep a job for very long. The family was barely getting by. Then, the darkest time came when Pleas was admitted to the hospital. Sally did not know what the family would do and was in great despair.

One day, she was in her kitchen when she noticed a sparrow in the house. No doors or windows were open and it would have been impossible for it to have gotten in. It did not act like a typical bird that found itself trapped in a house. Normally, they fly wildly into things and repeatedly fly into windows desperate to get out. This bird was calm and sat and looked around. It would fly through the house, into all of the rooms, and calmly land again. Sally walked to the door, opened it, and the bird flew out.

Almost immediately after the bird's visit, things took a turn for the better. Pleas' health improved and soon, he was back at work. Things were finally going well for the family and Sally could not help remembering her mother's promise to come back as a bird in times of need.

Aunt Nina

Everyone referred to Darlene's paternal grandmother as "Aunt Nina." She was everyone's "Aunt Nina." Aunt Nina could predict death. All of Aunt Nina's family knew that she had this ability, but they thought it best to keep it a secret. Aunt Nina claimed that she inherited this ability from her father.

When Darlene was about six years old, she asked Aunt Nina how she predicted death. Aunt Nina explained that when she first awoke in the morning, the person who was going to die would walk through her bedroom door, come toward her bed, and then disappear. Aunt Nina never saw the whole person, just enough to identify them. Aunt Nina was accustomed to these sightings and it seemed totally normal to her.

After Darlene knew how Aunt Nina predicted death, she began to watch for the spirits that came to Aunt Nina, but she never saw any.

In the early 1930s, Aunt Nina's deceased mother appeared to her twice. She said that both times her mother appeared on the side of the wall beside her bed and she was in an oval that looked like a picture frame.

As a child in the 1960s, Darlene loved the soft drink "Mountain Dew" and she also loved the hillbilly that was on the bottles. She told Aunt Nina that when she grew up she wanted to marry a hillbilly and live in the mountains. Aunt Nina told her if that was what she wanted, then she should do just that.

Darlene did just that. She married a man from Kentucky and moved to the mountains. Many years after Aunt Nina's passing, Darlene was at her home in Evarts, Kentucky. It was 1982 and she was taking care of her infant son when she began to smell a very familiar scent. It was "Evening in Paris" perfume which was Aunt Nina's favorite and the only perfume she ever used. The scent became very strong, but then slowly went away. Darlene knew that Aunt Nina had just visited her in her mountain home.

This story is about Darlene's maternal grandmother, Lona Amanda Moss Sandlin. This family was from Hartselle, Alabama.

Moss' Chapel

When Lona was a small child, her mother was stricken with yellow fever, a disease spread by mosquitoes. Lona's mother had been ill for quite a while. One day, she asked her two small daughters to go and get water from the spring that was located on their property. Lona and her sister, Nora, got a dipper and headed to the spring. As soon as they got there, a large red glowing ball arose from the spring. This frightened the children and they ran back to their house. They could still see the red light as they ran to tell their mother about what they saw. Their mother told them that it was a sign of death and the next day, Lona's mother died.

That property was later donated to a congregation so a new church could be built. The church was named Moss' Chapel. An old cemetery is still on the property where many of the Moss family are buried, including Lona's mother. People claim to feel "cold spots" in and around the cemetery and many say at night you can see white flickering lights above the old headstones.

There have been other reports of red glowing lights being spotted in the Moss' Chapel area. The lights are always seen immediately before or after a death in the community. Fifty years ago, a nine-year-old boy saw an eerie red ball in the middle of a road immediately after the death of a family member. About 75 years ago, two young boys were hunting and one boy accidentally shot and killed himself. The surviving boy claimed to see a glowing red ball after the shooting. As an adult, he contacted a physicist to try to explain the red lights. The physicist told him it could possibly be gasses, but could not explain why the lights are always at the time of a death.

In 1970, Darlene was at her home in Dowagiac, Michigan. Her grandmother, Lona, still lived in Hartselle, Alabama. One night at 3:00 am, Darlene was in bed asleep. She was awakened by something hitting her arm. She was not fully awake and began drifting back to sleep when she was hit on the arm again, this time more forcefully. The hit jolted her completely awake. She opened her eyes to find her grandmother standing above her. Her grandmother looked like she always did, except she was transparent. Darlene lay there without moving or speaking. Darlene could see her mother asleep in bed across the hall. Her grandmother turned and walked through Darlene's doorway and began gazing at her daughter, Darlene's mother.

Lona gazed at her daughter for a while and then she began putting on a pair of blue-and-white striped pajamas. They were the pajamas she had sent to Darlene's mother as a gift. She buttoned them from bottom to top and once they were completely buttoned, she turned to look at Darlene and then back at Darlene's mother once more. Then, she slowly disappeared. Darlene knew that her grandmother had died. She never went back to sleep.

A few hours later, it was time to get ready for school. She told her mother what had happened and that she was certain her grandmother had died. Her mother told her that it was a nightmare and that everything was fine.

Darlene was waiting for the school bus in her front yard when she heard the phone ring. It was her family in Alabama telling that her grandmother had passed away at 3:00 am that morning. Later that day, Darlene went into her mother's room and opened her dresser drawer. The blue-and-white striped pajamas were folded neatly in the drawer.

The Eighteen-Wheeler

In June of 1971, Darlene's husband, Butch, her sister-in-law, Luada, Luada's husband, Royce, and Royce's sister, Cleta, were all traveling from Dowagiac, Michigan, to Evarts, Kentucky. Cleta had been staying in Michigan, and the other three had gone to bring her back home to Kentucky.

The four left Dowagiac late in the evening in Butch's 1969 navy blue Ford LTD. They had been traveling about three hours and were in Indiana when everyone but Butch, who was driving, decided to take a nap. Butch was traveling on a two lane country road when he became very drowsy. Despite his efforts, he soon dozed off.

The car was crossing the center lane when all four of the occupants of the car were jolted awake by the sound of a blasting horn. They awoke to the sight of a huge eighteen wheeler coming right at them. Its bright headlights were only inches from the front of their car. It was too late to avoid it, so everyone prepared themselves for a horrible crash. At the moment when there should have been a tremendous impact, there was nothing. All four say that the eighteen-wheeler literally passed through the car like a huge mist.

Had the truck hit the much smaller car head on, all four would have most definitely perished. Butch's parents would have lost two of their children, Royce's parents would have lost two of their children, and Darlene would have been left a young single mother with a fatherless child. Darlene and her family are all thankful for the miraculous event that happened that summer night.

This was one of my son's personal favorites and he spoke of it frequently. As an eight-year-old, he talked about the "electric man" as if it were a robot or something out of a science fiction movie. When I heard the description of the "electric man," I imagined a man glowing from within to the point that his blood vessels were visible.

The Electric Man

Darlene was only four years old when this happened, but she can still remember it. It was in the late 1950s, and she and her family lived out in the country in Dowagiac, Michigan. It was about dusk one evening and her mother walked over to the door and began peering out of its window. She immediately jumped back and screamed. Everyone rushed to her and asked her what was wrong. She claimed that, when she looked out of the window, she saw what she described as an "electric man."

She said that right outside the door was a man who was all lit up. His eyes were red and glowing and he had wires running through his entire body. Darlene said that her mother frequently talked about this event. No one can really be certain of what it was, but she truly believed she saw an "electric man."

Caroline
From The
Journal Of
James Saylor

Introduction

The year 1969 was a time of war, peace, revolution, protest, freedom, and self-expression. Young people were desperate to be heard and felt empowered by living their lives much differently than their parents had in the generations before. The hippie era was well under way by 1969 and had spread throughout the country. Some young people traveled a different path and served their country in Vietnam. Some did both; some did neither. No one can deny that 1969 was a time of change that symbolized a loss of innocence for many and in many different ways. Harlan County, Kentucky was no exception.

Harlan County wasn't like the rest of the nation at the beginning of 1969. It, as well as much of the Appalachian Mountain region, hadn't "caught up" with the rest of the country. Although greatly affected by the Vietnam War, it was very secluded and many mountain people still lived the "old way." Most people didn't own phones or televisions, and to some they were considered a luxury, while others considered them foolish. Not everyone owned a car and many so-called county highways were simply horse paths with fresh gravel poured over them to allow an occasional car to pass through. Some still lived without the convenience of electricity. The people who lived near the city of Harlan were more up to date than their neighbors who dwelled in the mountains and hollows. Nonetheless, all the residents of southeastern Kentucky were separated from the rest of the nation by tall mountains and vast wilderness.

Harlan County had gained great fame in the '20s, '30s, and '40s by a huge coal mining boom. The feuds that resulted from this boom made the terms "Harlan County Wars" and "Bloody Harlan" well-known nationally. By 1969, things had calmed down greatly and coal mining was at a slower but consistent level. No one knew that just around the corner would be a "bigger boom" of the 1970s that would put Harlan back in the limelight for a while.

Death and murder were not rare in Harlan County. It had seen its share of bloodshed over the years. When a murder took place, it was during a fight of some sort. The victim and murderer usually knew one another. There was a dispute involved or perhaps revenge played a hand. The murderer may have been carrying out a biblical phrase that was considered law in the mountains: "An eye for an eye…" Many a family feud went on for years as result of this "law."

Alcohol caused many murders in Harlan. Too much moonshine made emotions run high and rational thinking run low. Many young men sobered up to realize they had killed a friend or brother over something ridiculous.

Everything in the mountains had a code of ethics and murder was no exception. Most believed it was a deed to be carried out in an honorable fashion. Your victim would know why he or she was being killed and who was doing it. The murderer was prepared to face the consequences and the act was usually carried out in public and in broad daylight. There was no need to be sneaky about it and you never preyed on the young; you protected them. You didn't leave a corpse exposed; you buried it.

That is why the event that took place in June 1969 was so important. It had such an impact on the people of Harlan because it was not their way. It couldn't be one of their own. Could it? It must have been an outsider. It had to be someone who quietly crept into the sanctity of the mountains to commit this evil. Was it? All that anyone knew for sure was that a monster, at some point, was among them and did the unthinkable. Was he still there?

The following is an account of the events from 1969 to present. Much of it is from a journal by James Saylor regarding his experience that is directly related to this event.

Unidentified Girl

On Sunday, June 1, 1969, the body of a young girl was discovered on the Little Shepherd Trail on Pine Mountain in Harlan County, Kentucky. The body was found about 50 feet off the trail. The badly decomposed body was nude and had a stab wound to the chest. The body was found by a Cumberland, Kentucky man who claimed he was picking flowers for his wife when he discovered the body.

The coroner at the time, Dr. Philip Begley, said that the body was badly deteriorated and identification would be difficult. He said the girl was less than 20 years of age, about 5'3" with a medium build, and reddish blonde hair. He stated she had been dead two or three weeks. Near the body, a woman's blouse and a man's sweater were found. There was also an order ticket from a Cincinnati, Ohio restaurant found close to the body. The police said they believed she had been murdered elsewhere then dumped where she was found. Coroner Begley said, that due to the condition of the body, it was impossible to tell if she had been raped.

An investigation began to find the girl's identity. Harlan County authorities had never encountered such a crime. There were no such things as DNA testing and national databases at that time. Being in such a remote area, there was very little press coverage of this crime. This case did not make national news and it is doubtful it made statewide news. It is possible that a Lexington, Kentucky television station covered the story and possibly, some other southeastern Kentucky newspapers covered it. State Police claimed their leads were coming from local sources, other parts of the state, and from other states as well. More than likely, the other states they were referring to were Virginia and Tennessee whose borders are very close by. There is never any mention in the local newspaper of a murder investigation although there was one. The identity of the girl was the main focus of the investigation.

A local funeral home, Colonial Chapel, took possession of the body and prepared it for visitation. The visitation was supposedly for people to come and see if they recognized the girl. It turned out to be a tourist attraction of sorts and a social event. According to witnesses, people were lined up out the door to try to see the girl's body as if they were at a carnival attraction or a spook house. The next day, a simple funeral was held and the burial took place in the Harlan Gas Cemetery, Harlan, Kentucky. There was no more media coverage after that.

People were talking among themselves. There was a lot of whispering and finger-pointing. The man who discovered the body became a local hero for a while. Even though the local newspaper never mentioned the murder after the girl's burial, the locals didn't stop talking about it. Everybody had their own theory and rumors were flying. People were talking about it in their homes and with their friends. This was the biggest thing to hit Harlan County in years, plus, it was the first murder of this kind to ever take place in the area. To top it off, there were two colossal questions that were unanswered: Who was she? Who killed her? No one could answer these questions.

It seems that this case quickly goes from murder, to open case, to cold case, and then finally, by the mid-1970s, it was legend. People were still talking about it, but now around campfires. It was now a story that was used for entertainment and scaring kids. It seemed to turn into an urban legend. Because of this, it didn't seem real to the listeners, especially the ones who didn't recall the event themselves. People would stop while picking berries or hunting on Pine Mountain and point out the spot where she was found. Some would make a special trip to the spot as if they were drawn to it out of morbid curiosity. Others would go and visit the grave. It wasn't forgotten, it just took on a whole new personality. Maybe if it all were solved it wouldn't be quite so fun to talk about. Knowing her and her killer's identities would spoil everything.

The young victim of this heinous crime has been called several things: Unidentified Girl, Harlan County Jane Doe, and Little Shepherd Trail Girl. For reasons that will be explained later, from this point on, she will be called "Caroline."

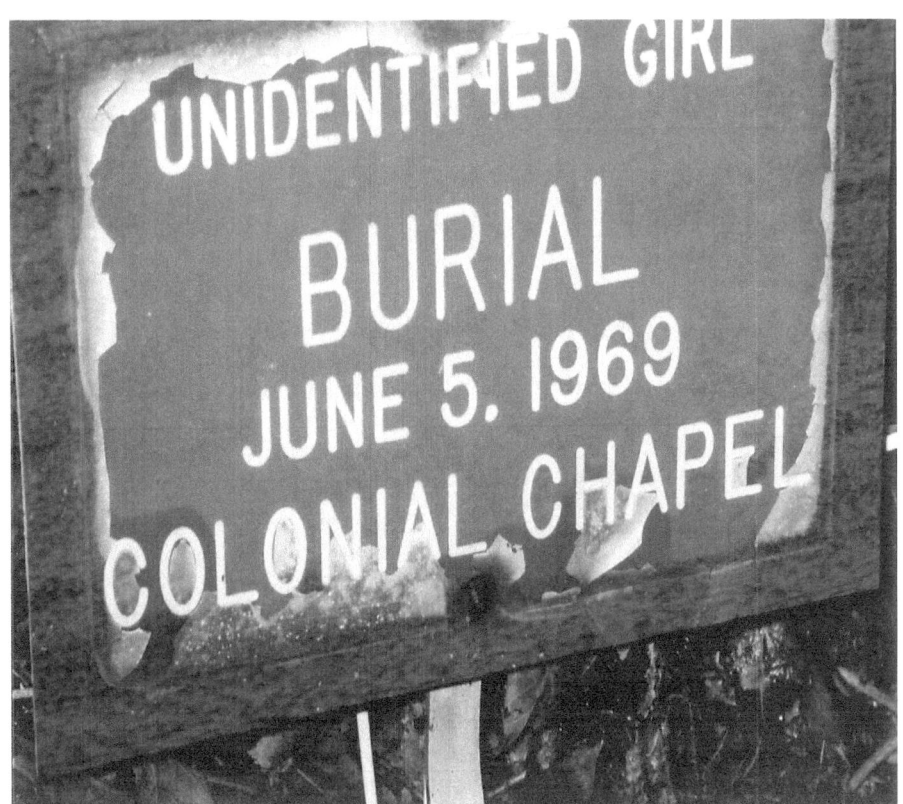

Found On Pine Mountain

Identity Of Murdered Girl Still A Mystery

Authorities were without a lead today as to the identity of a girl whose nude body with a stab wound in the chest was found about noon yesterday along the Little Shepherd Trail on top of Pine Mountain

State Police said they were checking out missing persons reports from surrounding areas as fast as they are received, but have come up with no clues as to her identity.

Coroner Dr. Philip J. Begley said today that the body was badly deteriorated, making identification difficult.

He described the girl as being under 20 years of age, white, about 5'3" tall, of medium build and with reddish-blond hair. She had been dead "at least two or three weeks," he said.

A few articles of clothing were found near where the body was discovered, Dr. Begley added, and an order ticket from a Cincinnati, O., restaurant was also nearby. Police were making an effort to learn whether there was any connection between the girl and the ticket.

Reuben Rice of Cumberland, the Democratic nominee f o r constable, district three, found the body.

Rice said today that he had gone on the mountain to look for wild flowers for his wife.

When he pulled to the side of the Little Shepherd Trail about a mile north of the Laden Trail, he said, he saw a blouse and man's sweater on the ground ' down the bank" from where he had parked.

"I was curious and went over to take a look at them," Rice said, "and, as I started to turn back to the car, I saw the body on down the hill."

State Police believe the girl was killed elsewhere and then dragged to the spot about 50 feet off the trail where Rice found her.

Dr. Begley said it was not possible because of the condition of the body to determine whether or not she had been raped.

U.S. Casualty

June 2, 1969, Harlan Daily Enterprise

Girl's Identity Police Checking Leads On Dead

State Police are checking out "numerous leads" in an effort to identify the slain girl whose body was found on top of Pine Mountain Monday.

Some leads are coming from local sources, a State Police spokesman said, but most are coming from elsewhere in the state and other states.

The girl, described as probably in her late teens, had been dead at least two to three weeks when her body was discovered by a Cumberland man about 50 feet off the Little Shepherd Trail, Coroner Dr. Philip J. Begley said. She had a stab wound in the chest.

The body is at Colonial Chapel pending identification.

June 3, 1969, Harlan Daily Enterprise

Stab Victim Is Buried Unidentified

The body of a young girl found four days ago on Pine Mountain with a stab wound in her chest was buried here today, but authorities still have been unable to identify her.

The burial took place in Harlan Gas cemetery with members of the Harlan County Rescue Squad serving as pallbearers. Colonial Chapel handled the arrangements and the Rev. Brian Ragan officiated.

State Police said today they are still getting calls from persons in and out of state concerning possible identity of the girl and they are checking out all leads available.

The girl, whose nude body was found about 50 feet off the Little Shepherd Trail by a Cumberland man looking for wildflowers, had been dead at least two to three weeks when she was found, Coroner Dr. Philip J. Begley said.

Several out-of-county people have come in during the past couple of days in an effort to identify the body.

Harlan Daily Enterprise Photo

Who Was Caroline?

There are few facts about who Caroline was. She was very young, probably born between 1948 and 1955. She was a rather small person. She was white or appeared white. The articles of clothing found with her do not give many clues. Without a description of the blouse, it does not offer any information. Every female, at some point, owns a blouse, if not several. What color was it? What style was it? Did it have tags? Was it high quality or in very ragged condition? Where was the rest of Caroline's clothing? Even though she was found nude, only a blouse was found at the site where the body was discovered. Why was only the blouse there? A man's sweater was there. A sweater in June in Harlan? Even at night, it is rare to need a sweater in the late spring in the south. Had she been wearing a man's sweater as a sign of affection? Had her killer been wearing it because he was cold? Could they have just arrived from somewhere north?

Possibly, someone involved had been in Cincinnati, Ohio at a restaurant. Why was an order ticket found with the body? Why were any of these things found there? It seems the killer or killers were careless or never imagined them ever being found. It does not appear that they were playing games with the police as many criminals do. Whoever put her there assumed she and the items would never be found. It was probably dark when Caroline was dragged off of the trail. Things can fall out of cars and pockets when someone is in hurry, but not 50 feet away from the trail. The clothing was probably tossed out with her and the order ticket may have been an accident. Someone could have become very hot and sweaty after carrying a body 50 feet and no longer had need of a sweater.

Caroline had to have bled severely due to her stab wound. Did the person dragging her get blood on their sweater? Did they throw down the sweater because they could not be seen with blood all over them? Had she been in the trunk of a car? Could anyone drag a body 50 feet by themselves? Caroline was small, but there is a reason for the term "dead weight." Even a person her size would be difficult for someone to drag or carry that far by themselves.

Who could Caroline have been? She could have been a wide-eyed teen who just fell in love with the man of her dreams. Her parents didn't approve, for good reason, and she ran away with him. Things went horribly wrong and she met her demise at the hands of her new love.

Caroline could have been a newly transformed hippie exploring and testing the waters. She could have been hitchhiking, as many did in those days, and willingly hopped into a strange vehicle for a road trip. She could have been hitchhiking and forcefully put into a strange vehicle.

Caroline could have been a daughter desperate to rebel and be her own person; someone ready to meet new people and have a new life. Caroline could have been no one's daughter; an orphan on her own much of her life and seeking attention from anyone who would give it. Caroline could have been escaping a violent situation only to find herself in another. Caroline could have been a girlfriend, prostitute, or secret lover.

Did she know too much or was she in the wrong place at the wrong time? Did she lie about her age? Was her murder considered a necessity? One thing that Caroline was, for sure, was a victim. No matter who or what she was, she did not deserve the viciousness bestowed upon her.

Did someone look for Caroline? Is someone still looking for Caroline? Were people sick with worry and grief? Were they angry, thinking she had left them for a better life? Are they still angry? Do they think she is living it up in Mexico or California? Did her absence go unnoticed? Could someone be that invisible? Someone had to have known or missed this young girl. If Caroline was from the north, someone finding her in Harlan would have been like finding a needle in a haystack. It would have been impossible. No one who cared knew she was going to Harlan County. Did anyone know she was going to Harlan?

Grave of Unidentified Girl, Harlan Gas Cemetery

James

The years went on. People who were alive at the time of the 1969 murder were getting older. The kids who heard about it in the '70s were adults and the kids of the '80s and '90s had never heard about it. Caroline was either a vague memory or nonexistent. By the year 2000, people were too concerned about their future to remember the past.

James was much the same way. The year 2000 found him a free man. He was divorced and his children were grown. He was planning a new life for himself. He was preparing to start over in a new place.

"*This spring in the year 2000, I decided I would go west, maybe northwest. In April, I left Harlan County. I was thinking of settling in Canada or maybe even Alaska. After three weeks of travel and rubber-necking, I found myself in Greeley, Colorado. The high cost of gas and motels were taking their toll financially. I wasn't broke, but I realized Canada or Alaska was no longer an option. Also, the weather was worse than I expected and it was still winter in Colorado. I could imagine how cold it was in Alaska! I returned home to Kentucky.*"

Disillusioned, James came back home to the mountains. James Edward Saylor had lived most of his life in Harlan County. He made his living as a construction worker running heavy equipment. He raised a family doing this. He was from a family who was about three generations deep of Harlan County natives. He did not come from rich people. He came from hard working people. He came from a family of Cherokee descent.

His grandmother was a proud Cherokee woman, as was his mother. He came from a family that had lived in the mountains for many years. James was a good-looking man who was spontaneous and intelligent. He was artistic and creative. There are many words to describe James, but the word "psychic" never comes to mind.

James arrived back in Harlan to face the reality that he had let his apartment go and had sold or given away all of his belongings. He had nothing and nowhere to go. The two motels in Harlan were full. He stopped by to visit an old friend. His friend asked him where he was staying and James honestly replied that he was going to spend the night in his truck.

"*Chuck invited me to stay at his house. Tempting as it was, he already had all the company that his house could hold. I told him that he was a little crowded and Chuck replied, 'Doesn't matter. You can have the other bedroom. These guys hardly ever sleep and when they do, it's either on the couch or on the floor.' I thanked him for inviting me, but declined. He then gave me an offer that was more appealing. My friend owned a trailer on the mountain where he was building a house. He told me that I was welcome to stay there, and I quickly accepted his offer.*

Since I had given away or sold most of my belongings prior to my excursion west, moving in was not that big of an undertaking. I moved in the last week of April and spent most of May cleaning and settling into my new home. The trailer was located about a quarter of a mile up the mountain on an old mining road that was called Red Dog Road. My trailer overlooked the city of Harlan. My soon-to-be nearest neighbor was the house under construction about an eighth of a mile on up the mountain. Due to the poor condition of the road to my house, I didn't have a great deal of company. I had gotten my trailer livable for the time being. I didn't have enough money to do any major repairs."

Soon, James found himself with nothing to do. He could do no more to his trailer for a while. Being raised in the mountains, he decided to explore the one he was now living on. He explored the hollows and ridges of his new home. He had spent much of his life in the mountains hunting and digging ginseng and was enjoying being out in the wilderness again. One day while exploring the wooded area behind his trailer, James realized that much of it was an old cemetery.

"I was surprised to find that much of the wooded area was a very old cemetery and I later learned that it was called Harlan Gas Cemetery. I wandered around it and noticed that most of the graves were not marked; a rock for a tombstone and a depression in the ground where a casket had long ago rotted and collapsed. I headed toward my trailer and right there, spitting distance from it, I found something that moved me deep within my soul. I stood there and read a small marker:

UNIDENTIFIED GIRL JUNE 5 1969
COLONIAL CHAPEL

I immediately remembered her body being found many years ago. As I looked at it, I felt a multitude of emotions. I felt an intense sadness that I had never felt before. She was just a child alone. Whoever she was, she did not deserve this. She was somebody's child. What kind of nightmare must her parents' lives have been and maybe still are. I guess to understand how I felt you would have to have a daughter and love her as much as I do mine."

James had never been a believer in the supernatural of any kind. He was not interested in it, but perhaps the sincerity of his sadness made a connection with this young girl's spirit. Whatever the reason, James was encountered by this young girl.

"A couple of days later in the early morning hours, something awakened me. It was not a sound, but more of a presence. I sat up and looked around my room. I immediately saw a young woman there. She was not a wisp, a mist, an outline, or a blur. She was as clear as you can see anyone. She stood looking out the window. I slowly stood up and began to approach her. When I did, she disappeared. I only saw her left profile. She never looked at me. She was gazing intently out the window at the

town of Harlan. Her face was expressionless. She acted as if I was the one who didn't exist."

A few days later, James saw his friend, Chuck. He told him that he may have seen a ghost. His friend chuckled and said "Yeah, right!" He asked what the ghost looked like. James told him that she was young, about 5'4", 115-120 pounds, white shirt, blue jeans with brown stitching, nice complexion, strawberry blonde hair, and not a bad-looking girl. Chuck laughed again and said it was probably the Unidentified Girl. He said he failed to mention that her grave was right behind where James was living. He realized James was serious and told him that there was a way to find out if his ghost is indeed the girl. He said there must be a description of her in some public record. He suggested a visit to the library and that is just what James did.

James began to search the Harlan Daily Enterprise archives. It wasn't long before he found two June 1969 articles describing the girl and the discovery of her body. He quickly realized that the girl's description and the girl he saw in his bedroom was a close match.

"*I showed Chuck the article that I had copied at the library. He didn't say much, but he knew that I had come uncomfortably close to describing the Unidentified Girl."*

James decided to try to forget about the unusual occurrence, but the thought of the girl that he encountered never left his mind. The fact that he had come so close to describing the girl that was buried right behind his home consumed him. He didn't know what to do about it or what it all meant.

The Message

It was now summer of 2000. Since he seemed to have quite a bit of time on his hands, James decided to visit a woman at Evarts, Kentucky he had become friends with. He stayed nearly three weeks with her. The third week, he began to miss his home, so he returned to Red Dog Road. Chuck had now moved into the house that he had been building above James' place. He invited James to come and visit his new home and James quickly accepted.

As James approached the house, Chuck's wife came out to greet him. She invited him in and he was given a tour of the home. In one of the bedrooms, James noticed some large carved doors leaned up against a wall. He asked Chuck where they had come from. Chuck replied that they were the morgue doors from Colonial Chapel Funeral Home. He said that he wasn't sure what he would do with them, but they were too nice to throw away. James asked him why he had them and Chuck told him that when Colonial Chapel was torn down, he had bought all of the salvage for building supplies. That was what he used to build his house.

On his walk back home, James kept thinking about Colonial Chapel Funeral Home. Where had he seen that name recently? Then he remembered. It was the funeral home that had buried the Unidentified Girl. He thought of what a coincidence it was that the place her body last stayed was practically rebuilt so near her grave.

James spent the next day in the city of Harlan catching up on things he had neglected while he was away. He arrived back home at the edge of dark. He put some groceries away and took a quick shower to cool off. Night had fallen. He went outside and sat in a chair by his front door. He was sitting enjoying the cool night breeze and listening to crickets. He was thinking to himself how good it felt to be home again. That's when it happened.

"*I'm just an old country boy. I love the fireflies and the sound of the whippoorwills and owls. Tonight was different, though. I heard an owl, but not like the ones I had heard many times before. I immediately knew something unusual was going on. There are owls in this area that make a 'hoo' sound and one that makes a mournful crying sound, but the call of this owl was intense or agitated. It is hard to put into words how I began to feel when I heard that owl. I felt a tingling sensation on my hands, arms, and the back of my neck. The feeling slowly spread to my whole body. It was very strong and for the first time since living there, I felt a real uneasiness. I didn't feel this way even when I saw the apparition in my bedroom. I sat there listening quietly and scanning the timber for a glimpse of this strange owl.*

The moon was bright and I could easily see the tops of the trees outlining the sky. I strained my eyes to look back into the dark foreboding forest. Finally, I spotted the owl. It was sitting in a poplar tree, right at the foot of the grave of the Unidentified Girl.

I sat there not moving a muscle and never took my eyes off of the owl. I thought to myself, 'We need to talk'. As soon as I formed that thought, the owl stopped making its eerie sound and flew away. I knew in my mind and in my heart that what was happening was not natural. I slowly stood and walked over to the grave. I spoke out loud, as if talking to someone I could really see. I said, 'Baby, I don't know what you want from me or how I can help you, but there's really nothing I can do without your help.' I stood there a few minutes more. I noticed something moving among the trees deep in the woods. It appeared to be a figure, but strangely enough, it was darker than the black forest. It was looming and moved very slowly. I couldn't tell if it disappeared or moved away, but I stood there until I could no longer see it."

James was not afraid. He just felt uneasy. The night was no longer pleasant and relaxing, so he went inside his trailer and went to bed. As he lay in bed thinking of what had just happened, he knew there was anger outside in the darkness. He felt it. He felt it earlier and he felt it now. He could not shake the eeriness that had taken hold of him outside. Sleep was not coming easily, so he got up and walked back outside. The night was beautiful and the hostility in the air was gone. It was peaceful again. James went back inside and was soon asleep.

The next morning James awoke and went immediately to the grave. Something happened last night that was unfinished. If she was trying to communicate with him, then he was going to try to communicate with her.

"*I asked her three straight and simple questions. 'Who killed you?' The name 'Philip Vanderpool' suddenly popped into my mind. 'Where are you from?' A place I had never heard of came to me, which was Fayette, Ohio. 'What is your name?' What came to me very quickly was 'Caroline North'.*"

James had never heard of Fayette, Ohio. It took him two tries on a road atlas to even find it. Fayette is a little town in northern Ohio, just a few miles south of the Michigan state line. James had been looking around the Cincinnati area because of the order ticket from Cincinnati found with the body. He had found a Fayetteville, Ohio about 20 miles northeast of Cincinnati and assumed he found the right town.

His feeling of success was short-lived. He kept getting the feeling that he should check one more time. As he picked up the atlas for a second try, it suddenly fell and when James picked it up, it was on the Fayette, Ohio page. From that point on, James was quite sure he was being guided by Caroline.

"*The next morning I awoke with a clear image of a man in my mind. The image was of a man in his early 20s. He was about 5'8" and had a stocky build, right around 200 pounds. He had thick black hair, a dark complexion with a square face, and dark eyes. He was possibly of foreign descent. He wore a checked shirt and a charcoal gray sweater with red and green designs on it. The man was sweaty and performing some kind of task.*

Then, in my mind, he turned to face me. This man carried no feelings of remorse or guilt. He was simply doing a job that needed to be done. I felt certain this man was Philip Vanderpool."

James concentrated on the name Philip Vanderpool. He asked around if anyone knew of any Vanderpools in Harlan. No one knew of any and it seemed that there was no one in Harlan with that surname.

It was now September, which is still a very hot month in the south. It was about 4:00 pm and unusually hot one evening when James decided to seek some shade. The wooded area was always cool and had a nice breeze. He wasn't there long before he found himself at the grave.

"I'm going to call her Caroline because I believe that just might be her name. I always think of her as a child. This year she would have been over fifty years old if she were alive. Because she died a child, she will always be a child."

James sat near the grave not thinking of anything in particular and enjoying the breeze that was blowing around the ridge.

"It's really not a bad place to be if you can get up and walk away any time you want. I truly believe Caroline doesn't want to be here anymore, though. She would like to go home."

James walked back to his home. It was cooler now, so he got a water hose and began to water his lawn. Then, he went inside to pour himself a glass of water. He turned on his radio to a local Harlan radio station, WHLN. The 5 o'clock news was on.

"I suddenly realized what the DJ had just said. He said that Philip Vanderpool, persistent felon, age 52, had just done something to someone, somewhere, and was in jail under a million dollar bond."

James got up early the next morning and headed to Eversole Street in Harlan. He was going to the WHLN radio station. When he arrived, he told the receptionist that he was interested in a news article that aired the previous evening. He asked her if it was possible for him to obtain a copy of it. The lady was nice and eager to help. She left and in a few minutes, came back with the original copy right off the Associated Press teletype. He thanked her and left. He was grateful that she didn't ask him why he was interested in the article. He wasn't sure what he would have said. It would have been a shame to lie to someone as kind as she had been. He had already learned that people give you strange looks when you tell them that you are trying to help out a ghost. He had learned that lesson at the library.

According to the news report, a man by the name of Philip Vanderpool had been arrested and was to stand trial for the attempted murder of his stepdaughter. He, his wife, and stepdaughter were at a lake in south central Kentucky swimming. The child began to cry and Vanderpool held her head underwater to the horror of many eye-witnesses. Was it just a coincidence that a very violent man named Philip Vanderpool was living in Kentucky? He was described as a persistent felon. His age was 52, making him a young man, about 22, in 1969. It all fit like a pieces of a bizarre puzzle.

James wasn't sure what he would do if he did indeed find a piece of solid evidence linking Vanderpool to the murder or if he found a missing person by the name of Caroline North. Would he approach authorities? He would probably be arrested on the spot or at least made a suspect. Would he be forced to take some sort of mental examination? Would he pass?

James got some help from friends who owned computers. They searched the internet for missing persons, but came up with nothing. His son and one of his son's friends made an attempt, but, they, too, failed. While exploring the Harlan Daily Enterprise archives, James discovered that people from Harlan County had been in Detroit, Michigan in the spring of 1969. Fayette, Ohio is near Detroit. He also found that people from the Detroit area had been in Harlan. Some people in Harlan County, who seemed to have ties to the Detroit area, were arrested in

1969 on assault charges. Still, James found no connection to Caroline.

Little Shepherd Trail

James' lady friend from Evarts paid him a visit that September and stayed a few days with him. He and Geraldine cleaned the young girl's grave. They raked away twigs and leaves and put a small fence around it. They decorated it with flowers and an angel figurine. James had told Geraldine everything that had happened and she was immediately intrigued. She wanted to go to the place where the girl's body was found. James got directions from the newspaper article and they set out to find it.

It was a beautiful day and the Little Shepherd Trail was equally as beautiful. It was early fall and the leaves were showing a hint of color. James walked down below the trail. He looked back up toward the trail and his truck. For an instant, his truck was gone and there was a red-and-white car sitting in its place. He thought his eyes were playing tricks on him and quickly dismissed it. He continued to walk on around the hill. Geraldine was above him on the trail. She said something and he looked up. Once again, his truck was replaced by the same red-and-white car.

"*I said, 'Gerl, I see a shiny red-and-white car. It is either new or has just been waxed. Its trunk is up and there is something lying between the trunk and the rear windshield. It is the same color as the car, but I can't tell what it is'. 'You may be standing where she was found,' Geraldine said, trying to find a reason for this occurrence. That was September, 14, 2000 at about 3:00 pm. We left shortly after that and went home.*"

That evening, James and Geraldine decided to take some photographs of Caroline's newly cleaned grave. Geraldine had a camera, so they bought film and began snapping photographs of the grave and wooded area around it. James had been watching Geraldine take the photos and decided he would give it a try. He took a photograph of the grave. A large glowing light fills up most of the photograph.

Photograph courtesy of James Saylor

James began to think more about his trip to the Little Shepherd Trail. He wondered about the red-and-white car he saw. Was that the car that brought Caroline to the Little Shepherd Trail? Was she killed in that car or was her dead body put in it to transport it? Was Caroline riding this car when she arrived in Harlan County?

James decided he needed to visit the Little Shepherd Trail again. This time, he needed to be alone. He went back a few days later. James was not sure where the body was found. He used the newspaper article for help with directions. It said she was found about a mile off of Laden's Trail on Little Shepherd Trail. She was found 50 feet off the road. James took Laden's Trail to the entrance of Little Shepherd Trail. He then went one mile and parked at a wide place. On his previous visit, he had picked out a particular area where he thought she may have been found.

On this visit, he went back to that same spot. He said aloud, "Okay, I need some help here!" Suddenly, James felt an intense pain under his left arm. He thought he might be having a heart attack, so he began to walk toward his truck. As soon as he moved from the spot where he was standing, the pain was gone. James turned and walked back to the spot again. Again, the sharp pain came back. It was high up under his ribs. He quickly moved away and the pain was once again gone.

James was going to give it one more try. This time, he walked around for 30 minutes or so. He walked back to the spot once more and once more, he felt a stabbing pain on the left side of his chest. He quickly moved away and the pain disappeared. James knew what this meant. He was certain that Caroline was stabbed in her left side, through her ribs, and high into her chest.

The Girl

There is an old house at the foot of Pine Mountain in Harlan County. It is a simple farmhouse that was built many years ago. It is located very near the entrance of Laden's Trail. It changed owners recently. When an older couple found out the house was for sale, they were quick to act upon it. It was exactly what they were looking for.

The house was in good condition for its age and had enough land with it that they could have a big garden. It was out in the country where they could have privacy. The woman immediately called the realtor and made an appointment to see the house.

During the tour of the home, the couple was sure that this was the house for them. As the tour neared its end, the realtor asked if they had any questions. The woman asked, "Where did they keep the girl?" The realtor looked shocked and said he didn't know what she was referring to. Embarrassed, the woman quickly asked another question to change the subject.

As soon as they left the home, the woman's husband asked her why she had asked such a bizarre question. "I don't know," she said, "It just came out." She hoped the realtor didn't think she was crazy.

The couple bought the home and began making some improvements to it. They hired a man to do some minor repairs and remodeling to the upstairs. One day, the carpenter came downstairs and walked into the kitchen where the woman was having a cup of coffee. He very calmly said, "They kept that girl upstairs. They chained her up." He turned and walked back upstairs and continued working. The woman followed him and asked him to show her where they kept the girl. He pointed to a back bedroom. "Who was she?" she asked. The man said he didn't know and that the thought just came to him while he was working.

It wasn't long before the house's new residents began hearing things. They heard, what seemed to be, footsteps above them in the attic. They heard banging, loud crashing sounds, and sometimes voices. The sounds usually occurred during the night, but sometimes in the day as well. Most of the sounds came from the back upstairs bedroom and the attic. Sometimes, their children and grandchildren would stay the night with them. They heard the noises, too and pretty soon, no one would stay there.

Sometimes, there would be the sound of a young girl crying and moaning. The crying seemed to be of sadness and sometimes pain. The crying was the most disturbing. The other things could be explained, but when the sorrowful sobbing began, there was no explanation. It seemed the couple had bought a house that was haunted. It seemed that it was haunted by a young woman. They never saw anything, but kept hearing all these strange sounds.

Once, the sound of chains rattling came from upstairs. Other times, they could hear a young woman talking, but most times, they could not make out what she was saying.

Caroline? Is this you? Are you "the girl?" Were you kept in that house against your will? Were you murdered in that house? Once, someone was in the back bedroom and heard a young woman say, "Oh, this is a nice place!" Was it? Was it nice at first before the people you were with turned on you? Were you held prisoner and treated like a slave? Were you tortured for a while before being killed? Were you simply a toy that was discarded after someone was finished playing?

It is possible that the events that occurred in the old house at the foot of Pine Mountain had nothing to do with Caroline. It is quite possible that another young woman was held captive in that house. She could have been a mentally ill daughter that a family just didn't know what to do with, and was chained up to keep from harming herself and others. This story is quite interesting considering the close proximity of the house to the place where the body was discovered.

The police said that they believed that Caroline was killed elsewhere and then dumped where she was found. Could that old house be "elsewhere?" It would be interesting to know who was living in that house in 1969.

The Dog

James' neighbor had a dog. She was a young and friendly black Labrador Retriever. Her name was Missy and she was about a year old. Missy was James' most frequent visitor. James grilled out most every evening, and as soon as he put a steak, burger, or chicken breast on the grill, he knew Missy would soon be paying him a visit. She became such a regular dinner guest that James began making enough dinner for her, too. It turned into such a routine that one evening, when Missy didn't show up, James became concerned. James went ahead and ate his dinner and saved Missy's in case she was just late. He had already washed dishes and gone back outside to enjoy the evening when he spied Missy trotting down the hill.

Missy spotted James immediately and her tail began to wag wildly as she ran toward him. She was very excited to see him and was eager to see if he had saved her anything to eat. James was glad to see her, too. He was a little worried when she hadn't shown up at dinner time.

Suddenly, Missy froze mid-stride. She was only about forty feet from James, but she would come no closer. Her entire demeanor quickly changed. She began acting stranger than James had ever seen her. She was usually a friendly, passive dog, but now, she was standing completely still with the fur on her back beginning to bristle. She stood there, staring into the graveyard.

James looked all around, but saw nothing. He slowly walked toward the dog, but didn't get too close. She was a large dog and obviously felt threatened. For the first time ever, James felt as if Missy could get aggressive.

Missy's eyes began to follow something. James could see nothing, but Missy obviously did. He kept looking wherever she did, but he just could not see a thing. Missy began to growl and back up slowly as if something was approaching her. By now, every bit of her fur was standing on end. Whatever was coming toward her, she was going to try to stand her ground with it.

Suddenly, her anger and aggressiveness turned into sheer terror. She jumped back and yelped in fear. She quickly turned, tucked her tail between her legs, and began running up the hill to her home. While she was running, she kept letting out high pitched shrieks as if someone was beating her. Missy disappeared over the hill and her shrieking subsided.

James stood there totally alone in his yard. He still didn't move. He began scanning the edge of the woods to try to find whatever Missy was so afraid of. He was being very cautious. He looked all around in every direction. He then began to walk around his yard, hoping to find a snake or other animal that may have frightened Missy. There was nothing there. James knew he would not find anything. He knew his searching was futile. Whatever it was, the dog could clearly see and James could not. He saw where the dog's eyes were intently staring. Something that she did not understand was moving around the graveyard. He saw her eyes follow it back and forth. It could not have looked human because she loved all people. What she saw began to approach her. James could tell by her behavior. Whatever it was, she didn't want it to get close to her. She kept backing away from it. She considered it to be dangerous and ultimately became hysterical from terror. Whatever Missy saw frightened her so that she never visited James ever again.

Dark was now falling and James still stood there in his yard. He didn't know exactly what had happened, but he did know one thing. This was not Caroline. On the night of the owl back in June, the dark lurking figure that was blacker than the night was not Caroline. The evil, anger, and hostility was not Caroline. Something else was there; something else was in that graveyard. Could the whole side of the mountain have once been a cemetery? Could the spirits be angry because a house had been built on their graves? Could the fact that the new house was built from a funeral home have anything to do with it? James recalled asking Chuck's wife how she liked her new home. She said she loved the house, but at night, found the woods around her home to be a bit eerie. Caroline was not the only spirit in that graveyard and in those woods, but she was the only spirit James wished to communicate with.

The Lightning

It was James' turn to visit Geraldine. He went to Evarts and spent several days with her. Upon his return, he discovered that Red Dog Road was all astir. As his truck approached his driveway, his neighbors were already walking toward him. They seemed excited and anxious and he could tell that they had news. He quickly got out of his truck and walked to meet them. As he got closer, he could hear Chuck's wife saying, "I'm packing up some things and getting out of here!" Without even greeting James, Chuck immediately began telling him of a strange incident that had just occurred.

There had been some recent storms in the area. Apparently, shortly after a heavy storm, lightning had struck on Red Dog Road in a big way. Chuck had just come inside from working on his roof when suddenly a streak of lightning shot down from the sky and was so explosive that it blew him off his feet and sent him flying backward. The blast was so powerful and loud that surrounding areas had heard and seen it, and several individuals called 911. For a second, the whole graveyard appeared to be engulfed in flames. Chuck jumped to his feet and ran outside. What the lightning had done was unbelievable.

James wanted to see for himself. He and Chuck walked to the cemetery and James could not believe his eyes. Two large trees had been shredded into little pieces and scattered all about. All grass and vegetation in the area had been seared and was black and crisp. What James saw next was shocking. The lightning had bored right into a grave and the entire thing had literally exploded. There was a huge hole leading down to the casket. Dirt was piled on all sides of the grave with patches of black charred grass. It was all very surreal looking.

The exposed grave needed recovering and the gaping hole needed filling. Since James had worked with bulldozers for many years, he decided to do it himself. He rented a dozer and began refilling the grave, doing his best not to damage it any more than it already was. James had also worked with explosives most of his life, and he could honestly say that he had seen few blasts as powerful as the one on Red Dog Road. The grave was once again covered, but the shredded trees and charred bushes stayed on as a reminder of the strange lightning that hit the graveyard.

The Farewell

"*Sunday, November 4, 2000. She appeared once, communicated with me twice, and guided my actions on several occasions. Once, a few days after she appeared, I felt her presence again. I didn't see her, but I knew she was there. I felt her in almost the same spot that I'd seen her in the bedroom. It was one morning and I had been awake for quite a while, but was still lying in bed. Something has caused her to leave and I don't feel she has ever been back. Not to worry, I have that effect on live woman, too.*"

James was doing all he could with the resources that were available to him. He was getting discouraged and realizing time was not on his side. Caroline's parents had to be elderly by now, if they were even still alive. People who were involved or remember the incident were getting older and dying. The possibility of finding this girl's identity was dying, too. As he sat on his porch one day, he asked another question, "Who are your parents?" The names, Roger and Patsy, were given to him. After researching, he discovered that there was a Roger North living in Ohio. There was also a North Street in Fayette that is not on the north side of town and does not run north to south.

"*You know, there must be restrictions in the supernatural world, too. Are they allowed to make contact with only one person and if it doesn't work out, are they stuck there, trapped in whatever dimension they are in? There were no voices, so apparently they can't talk. When I started slacking, she reminded me without hesitation that it was not over.*"

In late November of 2000, James' sister notified the Kentucky State Police about the information he was given regarding the murder. The officer she spoke with told her that if James was serious and believed the information he had was accurate, he should come to the Kentucky State Police Post and talk with him in person. It is hard to say whether they were interested or just being polite. One thing James found odd was that, when his sister told the detective where he had been living, he exclaimed, "Oh, the trailer girl!" She did not inquire as to what he meant.

In early 2001, James moved from Red Dog Road. He did not leave because of Caroline. He left because the water kept freezing and the road kept deteriorating over the winter. He had actually begun to enjoy Caroline and blamed several practical jokes on her. Once, he had found the base of his alarm clock precariously balanced on the top of the clock. Another time, the kerosene wick from his heater had been tampered with. He couldn't help but chuckle when he thought of these things.

"*It was sad the day I finished moving and came back to make sure I hadn't left anything. It was hard to say goodbye. I went out to the grave and stayed a few minutes. I came back in and sat down on the couch (it stayed with the trailer). I sat there for a short time, really hating to go. I began to hear a noise. The first time I heard it, I wasn't really sure what it was. The second time I heard it, I thought it was four wheelers going by on the road. The third time I heard it, I could tell it was coming from inside the house. I walked to the room it was coming from. A piece of plastic that I had used to winterize the window had fallen to the floor. The noise was water dripping from the ceiling and onto the plastic. The ceiling had never leaked the entire time I lived there and the construction of the roof made it impossible to hold water. There was quite a bit of water coming from the ceiling even though it had not rained or snowed in weeks. The carpet was absolutely soaked. I think she was sad about my leaving, too...*"

Acceptance

James moved to an apartment in the city of Harlan. It was very close to Red Dog Road. He could see the mountainside where he had lived from his apartment window. One day, later in the year of 2001, he looked out his window and saw thick black smoke billowing from the mountainside. He immediately set out to see what was going on and if his friend was all right. He discovered Chuck's house was on fire. Red Dog Road was far too rough for fire trucks, so there was nothing anyone could do. Chuck's house burned completely and the cause of the fire was never determined.

James had made a commitment to do everything he could possibly do to solve the mystery of Caroline. One thing he had not yet done was to go to the Kentucky State Police himself. In the late fall of 2001, he decided to do just that. He was apprehensive and really dreaded going. At best, he felt that the police would think him insane. At worst, he feared they may consider him a suspect. James' visit to the police department went better than he expected. He was treated well and found everyone to be polite and pleasant. Helpful? Not at all. It seemed that there were too many recent crimes to put forth any effort on one 30 years old.

James left things alone. No one wanted to talk about the murder case and no one wanted to help. He felt he had done all he could do and perhaps this satisfied Caroline.

Geraldine, James' companion, was killed in a car accident. She had been the most enthusiastic about helping him investigate, and after her death, he had not researched anymore.

In late 2003, over two years since James had looked for Caroline, she crept back in his life one day.

"*The reason I have started back on this is because, for the past few months, it has started creeping back into my mind more and more. Recently, some photographs of my son and daughter were rearranged on my table. I feel a presence, but not very strong; not like before. Still, I feel a strong need to continue."*

Once again, James seemed to be preoccupied with Caroline. He retraced his steps. He visited and revisited her grave, but came up with nothing. Her presence was never as strong since he moved from Red Dog Road. Sometimes, he wasn't sure if it was her at all. He considered going to Fayette, Ohio, but wouldn't know what to do when he got there. James never ruled out the possibility that Caroline could be from the Fayette County, Ohio area that is very near Cincinnati. Fayette, Ohio, is in the northern part of the state and is located in Fulton County. Fayette County is much farther south and the county seat is Fayetteville.

The year 2004 was spent simply going over what he had found before. He found some additional information regarding Philip Vanderpool. He also found a photograph of Vanderpool on the internet. Philip Vanderpool was convicted and serving time for the violent crime he had committed.

Even though he had aged 30 years, James was sure he was the man in his vision. Although this convinced James that Vanderpool murdered Caroline, nothing he found aided him in his investigation. Everything he found answered no questions. In fact, they just created new more complicated ones. It seemed he was at a dead end and this time, it was really over.

That year, James moved again. He bought a house and began working on it. Now that he was a homeowner, he began decorating and remodeling his new home and that occupied most of his time. He had moved into a nice, comfortable house and he really liked his new neighborhood. He still lived in Harlan, not too far from where he had previously lived. Caroline was slowly fading away. His change of neighborhood made all that he experienced seem far away and long ago. He was really moving on.

I first called this section the "conclusion," but that was not fitting. This is where all the questions were supposed to be answered. An in-depth investigation was supposed to occur.

Caroline's body was supposed to be exhumed and her body tested for DNA. The belongings found with her, wherever they may be, were also to be reexamined and tested. Caroline was supposed to be identified as well as her killer. Her family was to have closure and she was to have peace. Caroline was supposed to be taken to her hometown and reburied in the place that she called home. I hope to get the opportunity to write a conclusion for this story one day and I cannot help but be optimistic that I will. I feel that this story, in its current state, is so fascinating, and Caroline's voice needs to be heard so badly, that it should not wait to have a conclusion before it has readers.

I vividly recall the October evening in 2000 when I received a phone call from my Aunt Loretta. I was in the process of moving to a new house, but when she began telling me this incredible story, I dropped what I was doing and began taking notes. I kept saying, "James? Your brother? My uncle?" This was so out of character for James, I found it hard to believe at first. Although very interested and ready to solve a murder mystery, life happened and I was too consumed with moving to a new home and taking care of a small child to really do any research.

I, too, let it go until summer of 2005. That was when I was told about the old house at Pine Mountain. I immediately thought of Caroline and that sparked my enthusiasm. Then, my Aunt Loretta and I became more involved than we ever had. We searched and searched and came up with nothing. I expected to do a few searches on the internet and find a family searching for a daughter or sister that matches Caroline's description, but that was not the case. There are many families out there searching, but none seem to be searching for Caroline.

I have spent hours going over every "Jane Doe" network and cold case website on the internet. I have posted messages in the Fayette, Ohio, forums and basically exhausted all internet sources. This murder is not listed on the Kentucky State Police cold case website. The "Tent Girl" found near Lexington is a popular Jane Doe case and so is the "Lady in Black" found murdered outside a hotel in Harrodsburg in the 1830s, but no one seems to be interested in Caroline.

By the way, the old house at Pine Mountain was vacant in 1969 with the owners living in another state. It would have been the perfect place to quietly break in and spend a few weeks.

James and Loretta visited one of the last surviving people that were involved in Caroline's case. Joe Mahan, the previous owner of Colonial Chapel Funeral Home, lives at the Harlan Nursing Home. He has suffered a stroke, but his mind is still as sharp as ever. Mr. Mahan was eager to talk about Caroline. He remembered details of the murder very clearly. He had been the one who actually removed Caroline's body from the woods. He said that, when he approached the body, he stepped on the end of a stick. The other end of the stick was under Caroline's head and it made her appear to rise up. This was, of course, very frightening to everyone there. He said that he jumped in fear, and that it was such a bizarre sight to see a body in such late stages of decomposition look as if it was alive and getting up.

Mr. Mahan painted a very gruesome scene. James asked him how long her hair was and he said that it was so matted it was impossible to tell. He said her head was lying down hill. James had always felt her head was lying up hill. According to Mr. Mahan, Caroline's body had to be left in an outside building at his funeral home due to the overwhelming odor of decomposition. Joe Mahan told James and Loretta that he thought of the young girl every day and prayed that someone would identify her. He said that they were not the only ones still interested in Caroline, and that several weeks ago, another man and woman had come to visit him to inquire about the unidentified girl.

I saw Caroline one night. For years, every time I would think of her, I began getting goose bumps and a weird tingling sensation on my face. I would quickly divert my attention to something else. I began peeking apprehensively around corners, afraid of what I might see. I began sleeping with the television on and refused to get up at night for any reason.

Then, she finally caught me at a time that I could not get away: in my sleep. One night in a dream, a man walked up to me and gave me an old photograph. The photograph was of a pretty young girl with auburn hair pulled back on one side. She was fair with light eyes, and her complexion was flawless. She had a sweet look on her face, and the background of the photograph was blue and white like clouds and sky.

I did not have to wonder who this girl was. I awoke absolutely terrified. She finally did it. My worst fear had become a reality. She had made contact with me. I thought to myself, "Go back to James. He isn't scared to death of you." Caroline has not come back to me since. It's okay if she does. I am no longer afraid.

I have learned a lot while on my journey with James and Caroline. I have learned that until people have something tangible, they have no faith. I have learned that Caroline is one of many victims from the '50s and '60s that have never been identified. I have learned that few people filed missing person's reports prior to 1970. The biggest lesson that I have learned thus far is this: Once you let Caroline in, she never leaves. I have accepted this, as well as the fact that we may never know Caroline's true identity. My aunt, uncle, and I will go on searching with the knowledge that we will probably never find out who she is. We just want Caroline to know that someone still cares and someone is still trying…

now comes the night
when the hour is upon us
and our beauty surely gone
no you will not be forgotten
no you will not be alone

and when the day has all but ended
and our echo starts to fade
no you will not be alone then
and you will not be afraid
no you will not be afraid

when the fog has finally lifted
from my cold and tired brow
no i will not leave you crying
and i will not let you down
i will not let you down

now comes the night
feel it fading away
and the soul underneath
is it all that remains
so just slide over here
leave your fear in the fray
let us hold to each other
till the end of our days

and when the hour is upon us
and our beauty surely gone
no you will not be forgotten
no you will not be alone
you will not be alone

written by Rob Thomas and Matt Serletic
© Copyright 2006 EMI April Music, U Rule Music, and Melusic Publishing,
all rights reserved

www.ingramcontent.com/pod-product-compliance
Lightning Source LLC
Chambersburg PA
CBHW030507260626
47157CB00005B/1685